HUNTED

A HAVEN REALM NOVEL

MILA YOUNG

For more information, contact Mila Young.

milayoungauthor@gmail.com

Cover designer: Covers by Christian

ISBN: 978-1980366270

✿ Created with Vellum

DEDICATION

To my critique partners who never let me down and always
believed in my story.

CONTENTS

A NOTE FROM MILA YOUNG

I've had so much fun writing these fairy tale retellings and I hope you enjoy them just as much.

Each story in the Haven Realm series is a standalone novel and can be read in any order, though the more tales you read, the more likely you'll meet familiar characters.

These are adult fairy tale retellings for anyone who loves happily ever afters with steamy romance, sexy alphas, and seductive fun.

Enjoy!

Mila

HAVEN REALM SERIES

Hunted (Little Red Riding Hood Retelling)
Charmed (Aladdin Retelling)
Cursed (Beauty and the Beast Retelling)
Claimed (Little Mermaid Retelling)
Entangled (Rapunzel Retelling)
Wicked (Snow White Retelling)

More on the way…

HUNTED
A Haven Realm Book

Little Red Riding Hood. Three Big Bad Wolves. A Poisonous Scheme.

Scarlet, a healer, lives nestled in the forest surrounded by humans on one side and wolves on the other. But when a rogue wolf attacks her, she's rescued by another pack and taken deep into their den to perform her healing magic on an injured Alpha.

The wolves in the forest are under threat from a mysterious affliction, and Scarlet is the only hope they have left. Faced with a mixed pack of threatened shifters, Scarlet must use her wits and magic to survive and unravel the strange affliction now affecting the wolves... All while trying to navigate an overpowering attraction to not just one, but three of the Alphas.

Witches, wolves, magic and love intertwine in an exciting mystery that finds its own, unique, 'Happily Ever After.'

HAVEN REALM

The realms of Haven warred for ages upon ages, laying devastation upon its lands and its residents alike. To put an end to the death and destruction, the realm was divided into seven kingdoms, one for each race, ruled by nobility, entrusted to maintain the truce. Over centuries, kingdoms rose and fell as the power of the ruling noble houses waxed and waned. And the peace between the lands persevered. But a corruption is growing, bringing darkness to the realms, and threatening the return of war and suffering to Haven.

CHAPTER 1

"*S*carlet, get a look at him." Bee nudged me in the ribs.

I gritted my teeth, my hands juggling the jar of chamomile I'd just pulled off the shelf. "For the love of wolfsbane."

Honestly, Bee had the boniest elbow in all the seven realms of Haven. No matter how often I protested, she insisted on jabbing me right in the side every time she had something to say. Her idea of grabbing my attention wasn't tapping my shoulder but inflicting pain. I twisted around and my gaze flew through the arched windows of my store, Get Your Herb On.

A huge man marched out of the woods, arms swinging in an over-exaggerated motion. His chest stuck out, and with his chin high, I had him figured out in two seconds flat. I'd seen so many of his kind leaving the priestess's palace. Guards, full of cockiness and attitude, taking what they wanted without paying for goods.

Yet he wasn't wearing a uniform, but the strangest

clothes. A gray tunic falling to mid-thigh; no pants or boots. Goddess, his legs were the size of tree trunks.

"Who wants to bet his muscles aren't real?" I said. I'd heard of people using magic to enhance their physique. It was the latest trend in other territories.

Bee glanced at me with disbelief pinching her expression. With her braided red hair and ivory skin, most called her beautiful and always referenced her green eyes. But the real Bee was also tough. I'd once seen her scare off a bear with a glare, and there was a reason most in town kept their distance from her. Sure, it might have a little something to do with Bee insisting most of the folk were uneducated swine breeders—her words, not mine—but hey, she was a best friend who often popped into my store, and I loved her company. Even if she didn't know when to keep her mouth shut.

"How can they not be real?" Her gaze turned from the man and back my way. "He's not wearing pants. What could he possibly be padding—" Then her eyes widened, and her lips curled upward into a wicked grin. "You filthy girl, Scarlet. Never knew you had it in you." She whacked me in the arm, her strength intimidating, considering she stood five-foot-two and reached my nose.

"What are you talking about?" I slouched, a hip pressed against the counter, and pushed several sample bowls of tea leaves up against the ceramic cups that I had painted with different stages of the moon cycle. I called them my night collection series and regular customers tended to buy a new one whenever they purchased their regular healing herbs. If I had more time, I'd paint all the time.

"You're referring to his junk, aren't you? And well…" Bee glanced outside. "With the wind blowing against his clothes, there's definitely a healthy package in his arsenal." Bee wiggled her eyebrows and broke out laughing.

2

Fire scorched my cheeks. You'd think I'd be used to Bee's dirty mouth; after all, this was normal for her. "I wasn't talking about his... his privates."

Bee gripped her hips, cinching in the long blue tunica dress she wore. The outfit had a V-neckline and tiny buttons ran down the front. I admired her flowing sleeves, and I needed to re-examine my wardrobe. My black pants and sea-green blouse beneath the leather vest with a belt made me look more like a thief. But when I chose my clothing, I prioritized comfort. Most days, I lifted boxes at work and a skirt would get in the way.

"Just say it, Scarlet," Bee continued. "Dick. Cock."

I rolled my eyes. I had no issues with such words... As long as I didn't say them. I blamed my grandma, who'd brought me up strictly, no cursing or vulgarities. Heavens bless her soul.

"Penis." Bee licked her lips. "Blowjob."

A squeaky male's voice came from behind Bee. "Eww." Santos walked out of the storage room carrying several boxes. "I can hear you out the back. That's called sexual harassment of men."

I sighed, loathing that Santos had heard our conversation, and Bee spun toward my eighteen-year-old apprentice. But he might as well be fourteen with his thin frame, shaved hair, and his maturity level. Then again, were Bee and myself any better?

"Hey, men talk crap about girls all the time," Bee said. "What's the difference?"

Santos set the three boxes of tobacco leaves on the end of the counter. "You two are too old to talk about such things, and it's gross."

"Old?" Bee's voice climbed. "We're only a year older than you." She turned to me with a cocked eyebrow, expecting me to say something. I shrugged my shoulders.

"That's okay, Santos," I said. "We'll curb our tongues if it makes you uncomfortable." He worked his butt off, and I didn't need him leaving. He'd been working for me for a year and had just learned the names of all the dried plants we sold.

"It's fine." He didn't glance our way and instead opened the first box and scooped handfuls of tobacco into tiny satchels.

I marched to the opposite end of the counter. Bee followed me, probably ready to offer one of her smartass comments about Santos, but I jumped in first to change the direction of the conversation. "How come you're not wearing your new boots? The ones I got you for Christmas?"

Bee huffed. "Can't get them dirty, as I plan to wear them to the town ball. Might attract myself a prince in disguise. Besides, you live in the woods with lots of mud and—"

The front doorbell chimed, stealing her words.

We all glanced up to find Mr. No Pants bursting into the shop with a flurry, his breaths labored and his cheeks red.

"I need help," he wheezed.

The newcomer's attention fell on the three sets of eyes on him... mine lowering to his legs, and even with his tunic covering, he had a huge package. But I focused on the red bleeding through his tunic at his hip. How had he gotten injured? Animal attack?

At once, Mr. No Pants straightened his posture and flicked his raven hair over a shoulder, his sights sliding from me to Bee, then locking on to her curvy chest.

Okay, he was a womanizer. Score another point for Bee against Santos in the women versus men chauvinist race. The newcomer could at least have had the decency to keep his eyes above neck level.

Bee pulled the elastic free from her braid and fluffed out her hair. Typical. I nudged her and raised my eyebrows.

4

"Geez, live a little, Scarlet," she whispered. "You've been too sheltered."

I tucked a lock behind an ear. "Brown as a deer," my grandma had once called my hair. Nothing sexy about that. Maybe the reason I never got a man's attention was I stayed too safe.

My sights fell on the newcomer's blood. Was it a human who had shot him with a bow and arrow? I rounded the counter. "Are you all right?"

He stood at least six feet, with a solid square jawline, studying me as if I might be an animal he'd crossed paths with in the woods.

"You're injured," I continued.

The man didn't say a word, but scanned the room, and then looked out through the windows behind him. "I'm wonderful." Yet he stood there, a trickle of blood rolling down the side of his leg from under his tunic.

"Don't think so," Bee blurted out. "Unless you're a mutant who bleeds instead of sweating, you're about to dirty up Scarlet's floor."

He stared at me, and a brush of desperation shifted behind his eyes. The kind I'd seen when I'd first met Santos over a year ago, when he'd been sleeping on the streets, thin and pasty. Sometimes asking for help was the hardest thing to do.

"Come," I said. "We have a room out back, and I'll bring you hot tea to calm your nerves." I surveyed the dirt road outside and the woods in the distance for anything suspicious. My shop was located in the forest on the fringe of civilization, so I often saw strange things. But it was all clear.

A few weeks ago, in the middle of the night, another buff man with no shirt had turned up on my doorstep asking for specific plants for healing someone gravely ill. Before that, another man had been at my door, his clothes torn and his butt exposed.

Someone in the town of Terra had scored Get Your Herb On with a one-star on the town review board. The priestess ruling over the Terra realm in Haven had introduced a new system. The Customer Approval Plank, she'd called it, insisting it would assist people in choosing the best shops for their needs.

So now, not only did the scoreboard sit in the main town square for everyone to view, but some troll kept marking my store with one star. Was that person spying on me and noticing naked men at my door? No wonder my business had slowed lately.

Mr. No Pants scoffed and folded his arms across his strong chest, then cringed and lowered them.

"So, you going to buy something or—"

I cut Bee a glare, cutting off her words, then turned to the stranger. And I recognized the desperate need for someone to reach out and make that connection, offer a lending hand. When my grandma had passed away of old age, I'd lost everything. She had been my rock, my family, and without Grandma's support, her tonic soups, her hugs, I hadn't been sure how to go on. She'd raised me after my parents had been torn apart by a pack of wolves. Bee had reached out to me, guiding me to find purpose in life again, so now I'd do the same with this man.

"Come with me," I said and headed to the back, his footsteps trailing behind me. "Santos, can you show him a seat? I'll bring him some tea." Something to ease any pain he felt along with his nerves. Might even encourage him to open up about how he'd gotten hurt.

Without a complaint, the two vanished into the storage room. Bee shook her head, giving me a glare.

"Don't say it," I said.

I rushed to the pot of boiling water Santos had set up for samples. I collected a jar of valerian and arrowroot from the cupboard lining the wall behind me. Teapots, candles, and more tea containers filled the shelves. Together with a pinch of chamomile, the aromatic scents had my shoulders lowering.

Bee was in my ear, and I tensed again. "What if he's a guard? Do you want to bring the priestess's attention to your business? You know she abhors magic. That's why I do my enchantment spells in the basement at home so no one ever catches me."

"This is just an ordinary tea store," I whispered, lowering my palm over the tea bag.

Bee snatched my wrist and lifted my hand, sparks of white energy dancing across my fingertips. "Right, so this is perfectly normal?"

I'd always had the ability to enhance plants, and my grandma had taught me how to harness the power she'd insisted I shared with nature.

"It's nothing." I lied, well aware that the priestess who ruled over the human district forbade anything non-human related. And punishment came in the form of imprisonment for life. Each of the seven territories in Haven were homes to various races, from wolf shifters in our neighboring land, to mermaids, and rumor spoke of a girl with magical hair. Yep, one day I'd explore Haven, but until then, I'd remain in Terra with other humans, pretending we were pure and everyone else was the freak... according to the ruling priestess. And leaving Terra or strangers entering was prohibited. Hence guards captured any shifters or intruders in Terra for interrogation, never to be seen again.

"Don't kid yourself, Scarlet. I've heard the priestess infiltrated places like the bakeries in town, convinced their breads were too good to be true. And that the baker engaged in sorcery."

Her words left me jittery because I wanted to believe what I did benefited those in need. I drew on my ability to amplify the strength of herbs, so when people used them, they got the full effect. If chamomile calmed someone, then it put them into such a relaxed state, their anxiety slipped away. What was wrong with that?

"We'll be cautious, then," I suggested.

Bee nodded. "Smart idea. I'll be the bad enforcer and you the good."

"What? Wait, no."

Bee had already steamrolled toward the rear. I left the tea behind and rushed after her.

Santos appeared from the room, his attention sailing to the box of dried tobacco leaves.

"We'll be in the back for a moment," I said.

He nodded. "I've got this." He didn't seem worried in the slightest. Then again, he had no reason to believe the man was anything but someone in danger, and he had zero idea about my powers.

Once I entered the storage room, I found Bee leaning over Mr. No Pants, who sat on a chair, her index finger pressed against his chest. "Where are your trousers? This isn't a peep-show kind of store."

"Bee. Give him space to breathe." Without waiting for a response, I collected my medicine box from the shelf and flipped the lid open. "Now, let's examine your wound."

"How did you get hurt, hmm?" Bee towered over him, her hands gripping her waist. Geez, the girl should train as a guard.

"I'm not here to harm you. You can relax." He lifted the tunic up and bunched it at his side.

My gaze dove to his midsection like a desperate hound dog. Except the man wore black underwear.

Bee sighed.

He peeled away fabric stuck to the mess underneath, wincing, and I cringed at how much it must have hurt.

Three claw marks tore across his side, blood everywhere.

"Holy shiitake mushrooms," I said. "What did this to you?"

He cut me a strange look with a raised eyebrow, as if he'd pull away from my touch if I tried to treat him.

"Crapping balls, Scarlet. This requires a fuck me, not mushrooms," Bee blurted out. "But really, dude." She turned to the stranger. "This is bad. Like you'll die, that kind of bad. If you want my friend to cure you, talk."

Bee was the queen of exaggeration. The man only had a few scratches and would survive. "Bring me a bowl of boiling water," I asked her because tact wasn't her forte. I grabbed an old towel from the cupboard and cleaned around his wounds. They didn't require stitching.

"Don't listen to her," I said to Mr. No Pants. "What's your name?"

"Better you don't know." He didn't hold my stare, but instead studied the room, as if attempting to appear busy. Yep, right there was the warning Bee had mentioned.

"Look," I said. "I'm happy to help you, but are we in danger if we do? Do you work for the priestess?"

He scrunched his nose. "Gods forbid."

Bee returned with a bowl of water she set on the table, and I drenched the stained fabric before continuing to cleanse the injury.

"Where are you from?" I asked. "The mountains? The wolf Den? Oh, maybe you're one of those desert dwellers." The thought had crossed my mind. The human world was comprised of a massive town with several hundred thousand people. Farms dotted the outskirts, but this man wasn't a local. There was an air about him every girl in Terra would have sniffed out by now, especially if he was single. And I would have heard about it at the monthly town gatherings. The ones where the priestess reminded us of our blessing to be pure, along with the latest attempts by other factions to infiltrate our territory. In particular, Terra's number one nemesis, the wolves to our east. "Barbarians who attack anything that moves," she called them.

"I'm not from Terra." He held his head high, as if having nothing to hide, and his admittance didn't surprise me because it wasn't the first time someone had snuck into Terra for help. And humans did the same all the time, leaving behind our land and entering others for various reasons like falling in love with a lion shifter, or, at least, that had happened to a bookshop owner back in town.

"Are the guards after you?" I asked.

Bee gave me the *told you* look. But if you followed the rules, Terra was a safe place most of the time.

"No. There was a wolf. In fact, a pack chased me."

"In Terra?" I asked, squeezing the towel with my fist and returning to wiping his wound. I dabbed a mixture of my pre-made antiseptic onto his injuries, and he didn't grimace once.

"Nope. On wolf territory, in the Den. I was passing through and took a shortcut across their land and yours." He paused and wiped his mouth. "But a vicious pack found me and hunted me. I barely escaped with my life before they ripped my pants off."

Bee burst out laughing, her hand pressed over her stomach. "You sure it wasn't a pack of shewolves?"

He straightened himself. "Girls throw themselves at me all the time, so I'm guessing the wolves who attacked me instead of ravishing me were males."

Holding back the giggle in my throat, I placed a bandage

on his wounds and wrapped it around his waist, then tucked the loose ends in on each other. "There—"

A piercing hoot sounded somewhere outside, and my feet cemented to the ground.

"Fuck," Bee said. "That's the guards." She shoved a hand into Mr. No Pants' shoulder. "You said they weren't after you."

His face blanched, and he leaped to his feet, towering over us, his top falling over his hips "They aren't. But I have to go."

"Wait, you're still injured, and—"

He placed a hand to my mouth. "Hush."

I pushed his arm away. "Excuse me, who do you think you are?"

"Is there a rear exit?" he asked, his voice low and carrying an air of panic.

Bee stood in the doorway. "Tell us what's going on and we'll let you leave."

The man laughed deep and raw, almost terrifying. "Little girls, you cannot stand in my way. But I will leave you with a warning because you aided me. The wolves are at war amongst themselves. And one fight always spills over in other lands. I was attacked right on the Terra border."

"But we've got wolfsbane dividing our land. That'll keep the packs at bay," I called out as he stormed away from me and lifted Bee out of the doorway as if she were a doll. He then sprinted faster than anyone his size should have been able to.

Santos entered the storeroom. "Where'd he go in such a rush?"

Bee and I exchanged glances as dread threaded through my chest. I glanced out through the front windows and spotted two guards in uniform darting left. I sure hoped Mr. No Pants had escaped. It wasn't the first time I'd seen them chase trespassers in Terra, and, if I kept my head low, the guards left me and my store alone. "Well, he wasn't from Terra," I said. "No wonder the guards are after him."

"He's a looney." Bee wove her arm around mine and guided me back into the main area. "You should consider a lock on the door and only let people in after you study them through the window."

I nodded. She had a point, yet in the back of my mind, I couldn't ignore Mr. No Pants' warning. It wasn't the first time the wolves had attempted to claim territory. They had entered our land before my time, and hundreds of innocent lives had been lost on both sides.

"Do you think the priestess knows about the wolf war?" I asked.

"For sure. Otherwise, what else would her job entail? Oh, right." She cocked a brow. "Controlling all of us. Anyway, I should return home before the sun goes down. Do you have any wolfsbane?"

For those few seconds, Bee's words didn't register as I remained caught up in the whole wolves warring thing and the half-naked stranger in my store, who hadn't even given us his name. Perhaps a lock on the door to protect us from crazy customers wasn't such a bad suggestion.

Bee poked a finger into my arm. "Hello, Scarlet, are you with us?"

Shaking, I hurried to the counter and pushed aside the fabric underneath concealing the dangerous ingredients. Wolfsbane was poisonous, and I kept it out of view. I plonked the jar on the table, but it was empty and there were a few specks of dust inside. "Well, that's a problem."

Bee gripped her waist. "I thought only I bought the stuff?"

I scratched my head, then remembered where it had gone, but Santos stole my words as he headed into the storage room, calling out his response. "Last week, you added it to the concoction to clean the bird poo off the windows."

"Poo?" Bee paced to the door and back to my side. "But I need it this week. I'm hiking into the mountains to see a client. I assumed you had some." She leaned closer and whispered. "My client claims to have had a curse put on him, and I need wolfsbane to create a counter-spell."

Bee practiced magic in secret and was known for her abilities outside of Terra. Here, the priestess would arrest her if she found out, so Bee often sought jobs in other territories for her services.

"Sorry, I'd been meaning to top up the supplies. I'm running out of a few other things, too. When did you say you need it by?"

Santos reappeared with the bowl of hot water and bloody towel, heading to the front door to dump the contents outside.

"Tomorrow." Bee twirled a red lock over her shoulder.

"Sweet bolts, that's soon." I hurried to open the front door to hold it for Santos.

"Real sorry, Scarlet. It's just that I received the job this morning."

Santos interrupted. "I can collect some." His eyes were pleading, as he'd wanted to go out on a field excursion forever.

As much as I loved that he offered, I couldn't let him go. "No, it's all right. The plant's dangerous, and I don't want you getting harmed." Plus, I found if I applied my magical touch on plants while still fresh, their intensity worked a treat in spells.

"If it's too hard, I can ask my client if it's all right if we delay the appointment," Bee said, twisting hair around her finger, something she did whenever she was nervous. She

13

and her father struggled financially, and her jobs kept them above the water. I didn't want to cause them any more strain.

"You know I'd do anything for you," I said.

She ran over and drew me into a tight hug, her citrus and vanilla perfume bathing me. "Thanks. And I've always got your back, too."

"Sure do!" I giggled, and Bee broke away.

"Okay, I've got to go. Dad's finishing one of his new inventions, and I promised to be his assistant. See you tomorrow? I'll come in the morning?" Bee asked.

"Nah, I'll pop over to your place," I suggested. "You're always saying I spend too much time in the woods instead of society." For the past week, I'd been preparing a paste for her dad, who suffered from joint aches, and planned to finish it tonight to surprise him tomorrow.

Bee hugged me once more and kissed my cheek. She whispered in my ear. "Penis." With a giggle, she picked up her satchel from the counter and strolled outside with a wave at Santos before vanishing down the dirt track through the woods.

Santos returned inside. "Yes, I'll watch the place while you're gone. And I promise I won't make any tea pouches and only take orders if anyone needs one."

"You know me too well." I took my coat and bag from the back. Looked like I was making a last-minute trip into the woods. Yet trepidation sat on my shoulders, reminding me of Mr. No Pants' words about the wolves at war. So I grabbed a new bottle of citrus bane mixed with water. The spray would deter any predator coming near me, and, when sprayed in anyone's eyes, it made them temporarily blind, giving me time to escape.

CHAPTER 2

*O*nce outside the store, I shut the door behind me and feathered the red cloak around my shoulders. I glanced left and right, the hair on my nape shifting. No signs of the guards. Time to collect wolfsbane. I'd do this fast, as it was still midday, so I'd be back before the sun went down. But why couldn't I move? Mr. No Pants' words still whirled through my mind. I hadn't closed up shop when Grandma had died. And I hadn't been scared or run away when the townsfolk had protested that I performed the devil's work. All because I had insisted herbal teas could cure certain illnesses. Thankfully, the priestess hadn't demanded an investigation or trial. Regardless, a man who'd lost his trousers to wolves wasn't scaring me.

Grandma used to say having a soft heart in a cruel world meant you had courage, not weakness. And that motto had gotten me through the months after losing her and inheriting her shop.

Ahead of me, sunlight kissed the tops of the enormous beech trees with moss growing on their trunks, yet I rubbed my arms, fighting the chill that had settled in my bones.

Brown and green hues covered the field, and a dirt track snaked toward the forest thirty feet away.

With a glance back, I waved to Santos through the window as he continued packing the tobacco pouches. The bag over my shoulder bounced against my side in rhythm with my stride.

Trees surrounded me as I stepped into the forest. The sky vanished, and a red-crested woodpecker hunted insects across branches. A squirrel dashing up a trunk stopped and stared at me. *Cute.* A few leaves tumbled from overhead, and everything about the landscape reminded me of home. Safe. Familiar. Even a gurgling brook hummed in the distance, whispering in my ears. Grandma used to take me out hiking and hunting as a child, teaching me how to live off the land, and all about the freedom such a life offered.

Still, the earlier niggling concern about the wolves in our woods coiled in my stomach. I drew my cloak tighter around me and quickened my pace. The air grew still, broken only by the occasional birdsong. Woodsy smells calmed me, but, regardless, the pestering uncertainty remained, demanding I return home.

But what about Bee? If giving her wolfsbane meant she got paid and could help put food on the table for her and her father, then nothing was stopping me.

My steps sped down the sloping land. The dried foliage beneath my boots gave way, and I lurched backward, yelping. I snatched a low-hanging branch and pulled myself to my feet. "Crap!" I'd slipped down this hill before and worn bruises for weeks.

In the valley, a small creek gurgled, and the sun's heat beat onto my shoulders. Using the stepping stones, I hopped across, captivated by the pine smells.

Up ahead, the abundant trail of herbs came into view in a path dividing the woods and drenched in sunlight. The line of wolfsbane spanned the entire border between Terra and the Den, where wolves lived. People had sowed the vegetation to deter the canines from coming into our land decades ago. The line of plants reached my armpits and was crowded with long, dark violet flowers, each shaped like a helmet. Others were yellow and more potent.

A crunch of twigs caught my attention to my left.

I flinched and twisted around, expecting a deer, but nothing was there. "Stop being a chicken." Everything moved in the forest, from animals to vegetation. But when Mr. No Pants had run from the wolves, had they leaped over the wolfsbane and follow him? Unlikely, because they hadn't done so for years, so why risk getting sick now? It made no sense, and wolves were nocturnal, so they'd be hunting at night, not during the day. *Geez, relax.*

With a deep exhale, I turned back to the shrubs and glanced past them to the trees in the region called the Den. The wolves' homeland. The forest stood thick, like soldiers ready for war, with the sun barely penetrating the canopy. Each time I visited this location, I swore someone watched me. After all, I lingered near the border between our two territories. The wolfsbane kept them at bay... Yet my pulse banged in my veins as if I had made a mistake.

Refusing to think about anything else, I dug into my bag and plucked out the fabric gloves before sliding them on to avoid getting wolfsbane on my skin. Broken skin or wounds absorbed wolfsbane poison for both humans and wolves, but it killed wolves, while it made people very ill. I also took out the pouch where I stored the wolfsbane to keep it separate from my other herbs.

Okay, time to get started. I yanked the first plant out of the ground and dusted soil off the roots. A snap at the base and I tossed the top part of the flower down, as I only needed the roots. With a single thought, I called my energy and the faintest crackling of power sizzled down my arms. White sparks leaped from the tips of my fingers, through my gloves, and curled around the tuber. I placed the root into the bag and gathered three more from various spots to avoid thinning out the barrier in one area. Two to go. Bee always insisted on six for her spells, but, since I was here, I might as well stock up my supplies. I trailed along the shrubs, searching out the yellow ones amid the hundreds of purple flowers, when a loud creak sounded somewhere near.

I froze.

Then someone shrieked.

I rocked on the spot and squeezed the bag in my hands. *What was that?*

Branches and leaves thrashed in the breeze, grating and rustling.

Another screech. Louder. An animal in distress? With my belongings packed up, I threaded my arms through both bag straps and trailed toward the sound. Yeah, the opposite of what I ought to do, but the noise would haunt me for weeks if I didn't do anything about it. I pictured a hurt deer with a broken leg caught in a hunter's trap. I couldn't bear to see any animal hurt and would heal them if possible.

Or was a wolf attacking them?

I halted, chewing on my cheek, and removed my gloves, stuffing them into my bag. *What should I do?* I rushed forward and stopped again, swinging my gaze from side to side. Which direction was it coming from? Home was on the left.

Another scream, definitely a human wail. I darted right, targeting whoever was in trouble. Had wolves cornered someone?

Rushing closer, I spotted movement between trees in the distance. A man was on his knees, and another person whipped him. The victim cried, and I couldn't take another breath.

What's going on? I slid the knife out of my boot and crept nearer, using the enormous trunks to conceal my approach.

The weeping echoed, leaving me covered in goose bumps. I pressed my back against a tree twice my width, my heart racing as I listened to each dull whack. Every whimper and screech.

I peered out from behind my hiding spot. At least fifteen feet away stood a thin and lanky person dressed in black from neck to toes, complete with gloves. In her hand, she gripped a branch stripped of leaves and spiked with offshoots. I squinted for a better look, only to get a glimpse of her face: a long pointy nose and jagged cheekbones, along with thinned lips twisted into a grin.

The priestess?

Hair black as the night was pulled into a tight ponytail. When she smiled and brought down the weapon across the poor man's back, I cringed. In front of townsfolk, she presented herself as a lady, who, at sixty years old, needed a hand climbing the steps to her podium. Yet I'd heard rumors of her torturing people. Then again, all kinds of lies circled about her, from mating with aliens to bathing in milk most nights. Okay, maybe the last one wasn't that far-fetched, but at every monthly town gathering, others spread more gossip. So I didn't pay attention to them. But...what if they were right about the priestess? Grandma would always say there was no smoke without a fire when unpleasant things were said about someone.

Farther behind her stood at least ten people crouched over shrubs. What was going on?

"Will you disobey me ever again?" The priestess' high-pitched words pierced my ears.

I stood cemented. I had to leave without making a sound. For all I knew, this was some kinky sex act. Gross.

"Get back to work. Anyone else have an issue with touching wolfsbane?" she called out.

I stiffened at her last word. Why were they handling the plant? I mean, sure, I had for a legit reason, but the priestess didn't endorse magic or herbal healing. Was she collecting the stuff to create poison? Did I misunderstand something? *Right*, like her whipping a worker with a branch.

Unable to stop myself, I peeked out once again at the priestess. I had to see what the others were doing, as it could explain why Mr. No Pants had gotten attacked by wolves. I mean, I lived away from town, and if danger was near, I had to defend myself.

Darting from one trunk to another, I happened upon her again, watching over the ten people dressed in black. Each wore gloves and mouth masks. They carried full-grown wolfsbane plants across the current shrub border and headed into the wolves' domain. They entered the dark woods everyone was forbidden to visit. I gasped, at once pressing a hand over my mouth for making such a loud sound, and snapped back behind the tree.

What were they doing?

The crunch of a twig came from behind.

I spun back around. A guard had approached from farther away, and he'd spotted me.

Sweet mother of pearl.

The beefy man with no hair wore the gray uniform jacket with double lines of golden buttons. He shook a finger at me, as if I were two years old and being scolded by my grandma, and hurried closer.

Dread locked my stomach tight, and I wasn't sure I could move if I wanted to. I'd heard tales of the priestess locking up people she suspected spied on her. She was a private person and suspected everyone of doing something wrong.

The warrior's lip curled upward with a snarl, revealing

yellowing teeth, and his brow creased as if I'd just ruined his day by forcing him to do his job.

He reached for a long knife on his belt, because that was how guards dealt with anyone. Slash first, then ask questions. They obeyed the priestess' law and enforced anything according to her orders.

Heavens help me.

I rocked on my heels and swirled around the tree, running to where the priestess and her slaves worked. *Sure, Scarlet, go straight toward the person in charge.* Adrenaline fueled my actions, so logic wasn't part of the plan.

I leaped over a log and skidded across the dried leaves, arms flailing outward for balance. Landing on my backside had me wincing, not because I was helpless, but due to the pure shock of the experience. Fear turned my heart into a boulder, and I staggered up. I'd end up in a cell with no windows and rats gnawing on my toes. I lunged into a sprint, but in front of me another guard approached and the same problem faced me from my left. Escape lay on my right. Exactly where the priestess stood.

She turned toward the commotion—me.

I whirled on the spot, terror gripping me, and Grandma's voice sang in my head. Something about facing problems when trouble hit. How running away was not the answer. But admitting defeat was the worst decision.

My thoughts swung back and forth between giving in and explaining it was a mistake to escaping before I got thrown into prison. The priestess would suspect I'd witnessed her entering wolf territory, which was forbidden, even for royalty like her. Hell, she'd once punished a man who'd stumbled across her in the woods during her morning stroll. The victim had mysteriously vanished a few days later. Yep, everyone knew that if you kept your distance from her, you'd be safe. But now, I swore I'd witnessed something I shouldn't have.

"Get her," she barked.

Foliage crunched underfoot nearby, and a current of wind swept past, tossing foliage into the air. A large flock of birds chirped overhead, fluttering out of the trees in fright.

Sorry, Grandma. I darted in the priestess' direction, angling around her.

Her mouth hung open, eyes widening with shock.

Our gazes met, her nose wrinkling, and an involuntary growl rolled through my chest. Where had that come from?

Clearly, just the sight of her mouthing my name, *Scarlet*, had me acting all primal on her. She had visited my store before, searching for a relaxing tea concoction, as she'd called it. Her voice had been like a viper's strike when she'd stormed inside, and I'd sworn she had been about to order my arrest. But weeks later, I'd learned she loved my tea. Now, I doubted she'd be so understanding. Not when I'd spied on whatever she was doing.

"Stop her!" the priestess roared.

I careened around her, out of her reach. A torrent of air sliced past as she swung her branch to whack me.

None of her workers moved. But a strong scent of perspiration like I'd never smelled before smothered my senses, along with something metallic-scented. A worker bent over a shrub and the gashes crisscrossing his back stood out, blood seeping from the cuts. *Crap!*

My adrenaline soared as I charged toward the section where the wolfsbane grew, unsure where I was going, and why I'd decided this was a good decision. I thundered through the bushes, stomping them, and sprinted into the forest to where I'd seen others carrying the plants.

Inside the Den's woods, an eerie silence engulfed me, and chilliness bit into my flesh.

"Get her now!" the priestess yelled. "I want her caught."

Everything about today rolled through me. Basically, I kept making mistake after mistake.

Guards bulleted straight after me. I darted past more workers, who stared at me with frightened expressions.

I ran. Ducking under branches, leaping over evergreens. Weaving left and right to shake my pursuers. I never should have gone for wolfsbane. Or stuck my nose in. Or hung around after seeing the priestess whipping a person. Now, I'd be lucky to survive the day.

Around me, trunks blended into the grayish backdrop. Where was I? But I had to escape and work out a solution to my problems later.

Two guards still chased me, their heavy breaths labored, so I hooked a sharp left where the land sloped downward, speeding my pace. No stopping. No slowing down.

On my next step, I hit a dip and the toe of my boot snagged onto a dead branch. My world shuttered as the ground came rushing toward my face. I slammed down, the air thrust out of my lungs. I rolled down the side of the hill, screaming. Leaves and twigs poked my back; rocks stabbed at my sides.

Next thing I knew, I was airborne and, for those few seconds, I gawked at the sharp cliff I'd just flown off.

"Oh, shit!" I pinwheeled my arms, falling fast.

My screams faded in the rush of air crashing against me, ripping at my clothes, my hair.

I hit the water.

Iciness sank its fangs into me, freezing me at the core. Air bubbles rushed over my face. Tightness clamped around my lungs, squeezing them from the lack of oxygen. I thrashed my legs, not ready to die.

When my head broke the surface, I panted for air, waves

splashing me in the face as the current carried me downstream.

The river sprayed in my face, and I dog paddled, swallowing a mouthful. A sudden electric charge buzzed through me. I convulsed, my head bobbing beneath the current.

Time vanished fast, and panic hammered against my ribs. No one would ever find me and everyone would assume I'd gotten eaten by wild animals. But when the pinpricking sensation returned to my legs, I thrust them through the water, rising toward the sun-specked surface and gulping at the air.

Trees crowded the edges of the rapids on both sides, but my thoughts numbed as I battled the waters. A boulder rose out of the waves. I reached out and latched on to it, my fingers digging against the stone, my legs wrapped around it.

Each inhale shivered on the way to my lungs, and the coldness lapped against me. I stared back to the cliff I'd fallen from, so high, I could have died. But there was no sign of the guards. Guess there was one bright outcome. Yeah, right. I was lost in the Den.

Yep, great way to get yourself killed, Scarlet. Even if the priestess didn't imprison me for life, now the wolves will tear me apart. A paralyzing hurt spread through me, and every part of me twitched with the urgency to run, to do something.

Any other place and I'd love the location, the sun warming my head, the lush greenness, the snow-peaked mountains in the distance. Except I was in a tailspin of trouble.

The priestess would now visit my store and wait for me or, worse yet, arrest Santos. I'd landed somewhere in the forbidden territory—the Den—with wolves that apparently were warring. Oh, and I was soaking wet and had to get to dry land.

"Wonderful work, Scarlet. What's next on the to-do list?

Killing someone?" I shuddered at the thought. What was wrong with me?

"Okay, first get out, dry off, and get my bearings."

By some miracle, my bag had remained on my shoulders.

I stilled, listening. The hiss of a waterfall told me what I needed to know. Death awaited if I didn't get out of the river. Nearby, I saw another boulder, and yet another ahead, closer to shore. So I inched to the side of mine and kicked off, letting the rippling currents drag me to the next one. By the time I reached the third rock, exhaustion claimed me.

The stream passed me, and the cold cramped my calves. But salvation wasn't far. My head pounded; every ounce of my body screamed for a timeout. I swam across the river, water sloshing everywhere. Inches away. Almost there.

Pushing farther, I strained my muscles and fought the steady flow dragging me toward the waterfall threatening to swallow me whole.

With every bit of my remaining strength, I took long strokes, fighting the deluge.

When I clasped the lip of the shore, a new sense of vigor struck, but a torrent of water snaked around me, ripping me away from salvation. I yelped and swam harder than ever before. Always go against the current, I'd once been told, so I pushed myself as hard as I could.

The moment I reached the bank, my feet finally found purchase on the ground. "Freakin' hell."

I crawled out, trembling, and slumped onto the grassy field encased by lofty pines.

Every inch of me screamed with pain. Above, the sun eased my chills. And when I closed my eyes, I let myself believe I was safe, that I'd find a way home, that my world didn't balance on a knife's edge.

The last time I'd felt this lost and alone was when my grandma had died. When my future had seemed bleak. I pictured her smile, the way she'd always pinch my cheeks, then try to feed me six meals a day because I was too skinny. My throat thickened. There was so much I'd wanted to share with her, like how well the store performed, or how my new technique on drying herbs made the whole process faster. Whenever I'd had a problem, she had been my go-to person. My rock. Now... I wiped the tears running down the side of my face.

A deep guttural snarl carried on the wind. *Sweet bunnies.* I didn't want to glance up and find a wolf.

I couldn't remember how to breathe, speak, or move as terror ricocheted inside my skull. Bile rose in my throat. And, just like that, my situation got a million times worse.

CHAPTER 3

The growl came again, louder, and right behind me. I remained on the grass near the raging river, trembling. No mistake—the sound belonged to a wolf.

If I jumped back into the water and fell down the waterfall, it might be easier than being mauled.

Ice hardened in my chest. Breathing was close to impossible. I climbed to my feet slowly, all the while tracing the ground with my fingers until I touched a rock. With it clasped in my fist, I rose and twisted around.

The shaking wouldn't stop as I stared into the eyes of a wolf with steel-colored fur at least thirty feet away. The animal reached my waist and had seen better days. His coat was thin and hung loose on his frame. Just my luck, he saw me as an easy meal, and hunger would make him unstoppable.

One stone would be useless against him.

"I'm not food. I barely have any muscle on my bones." I sidestepped, figuring I could make a run for the woods and climb a tree. What other choices did I have?

When the wolf crept closer, he growled once again, his ears flattened against his large head.

I shuffled sideways, angling away and stealing glances toward the forest. A small tree with low-hanging branches was doable, because I wasn't becoming anyone's lunch, now or ever.

But from within the folds of the woodland, three silhouettes emerged, and I shuddered. Wolves trotted out in perfect unison as if they were warriors. One was black with cream paws, another gray sporting whitish stripes across the chest, and the third was pure white like fresh snow. They were half a foot taller than the creature between us. Shifters?

Perspiration rolled down my spine, and the thump of my heart vibrated in my ears. I squeezed the stone in my hand, fingers wrapping the hard surface. How was I supposed to defeat all four of them?

Panic churned my stomach into cramps. Before I could make sense of what to do next, I turned and bolted. All the rational reasons fell out of my head.

A strangled cry poured from my mouth.

Heavy breaths were right behind me, paw pads hitting the soil.

I ran faster than I thought possible along the river's edge. The cool air slapped my skin, pulling at my hair, choking me.

Bursting into the forest, I pounded the ground, foliage snapping and crackling.

Death. Not for me. Please, not for me.

A cacophony of snarls and grunts detonated behind me. I glanced back to see the three wolves in a brawl. Were they deciding which one got to devour me? But the white one thundered close to me, leaping over foliage.

I sprinted faster, ducking under branches and crushing bushes. Twigs scratched my face and arms. Everything hurt.

Something moved in my peripheral vision. I looked over, and my gut plummeted.

The white wolf lunged in huge strides alongside me, a few paces away. His head twisted in my direction, teeth exposed.

I threw my rock at him but struck a trunk instead. *Damn.*

Pushing my legs, I raced straight ahead and grabbed a low branch, then swung my legs up.

But something snatched my pants, ripping me back down, and my grip slipped. I screamed, grasping for the branch.

Instead, I crashed to the forest floor, landing on my butt and scrambling backward.

My life whirled through my mind. How little I'd done with the store, how I'd stayed in the woods as my safe zone, never leaving Terra. Bee had traveled to other lands. I followed the rules. Now I'd get eaten and no one would even know.

The white wolf stood his ground, while two of his friends trotted down the hill toward us. What happened to the first wolf? They'd defeated him to win the prize… me? The gray one tilted his head to the side, studying me, and trotted forward. Was he the alpha?

My feet itched, and I fought the impulse to jump up and sprint away, how far would I get?

I shifted to move past the tree at my back, but my backpack snagged on a root. And that reminded me of my citrus spray. I shook the bag off my shoulders and slid a hand inside. All three wolves watched me. Were they thinking I had a snack? The apple in the bag wouldn't sate these beasts. I wrapped my fingers around the small bottle with a cork top and took it out.

The gray wolf snarled, snapping its jaws inches from me.

I yelped and flinched sideways. "Okay, look. If you plan on eating me, then do it already, but clearly, you haven't yet..." I gulped and met his gaze when something shifted behind his eyes. He shook his head and released a low grumble as if trying to communicate. That prompted my next words. "Are you all shifters? And, if that's the case, well, you are being super rude by not welcoming me to your land." My rambling came from the panic slithering up my back, and I tucked my bent knees up against my stomach.

Silence swept between us, well, aside from the rustling leaves and gurgling river. What were the wolves waiting for? Were they trying to give me a hypnotic stare? Because it wasn't working.

A deep rumble came from the black wolf. Was it telling the others to attack?

When all of them followed suit and let out deep growls, I tensed and gasped for air.

Be brave, my little girl—Grandma's favorite saying. So I readied to fight to the end and balled my hands into fists.

The gray wolf twitched and charged.

Lightning fast, I scrambled backward and flung out my hand holding the bottle. But a wolfsbane root had wrapped itself around the broken cork top. Fumbling, I dropped my bag and the cork popped off, and the entire contents splashed outward, striking the gray wolf in the face. I threw the bottle at him.

He groaned with obvious pain and recoiled, shaking his head.

Mist danced in the air from my spray, and the black wolf sneezed, while the white one stumbled about.

On my feet, I spun and ran.

Heaviness slammed onto my back. My scream tore through my body like blades. I bucked and squirmed for purchase out from under his weight.

I shook, expecting fangs to dig into the back of my neck. I cried out, fingers grasping for anything.

But instead of biting me, the white wolf leaped off and seized my ankle. A primeval instinct took over, and I kicked his face. His lips peeled back with a threat.

I gritted my teeth, my breaths fast and loud.

"Help!" I ripped at plants, scratching my fingernails into the soil.

He hauled me like a trophy prize. When another wolf snatched my other leg, I writhed and bellowed. The gray wolf trotted alongside me, still shaking his head, and his eyes had turned red... must have been from my potion.

"Please," I pleaded. "I'll give you anything you want; just let me go." I seized a fist-sized rock when the big alpha snapped in my face, his bloody breath washing across me. Bloodshot eyes glared at me, and he kept squinting tight and shaking his head. But before I could toss the rock away, the wolf head-butted me. My vision blurred, fading to blackness, and the last thing I heard was a threatening growl.

* * *

A DOOR SLAPPED SHUT, and I opened my eyes. I glanced up at a ceiling in a dimly-lit room, a fire crackling nearby, its warmth cocooning me. Now this was the life... sleeping next to a fire at home. *Wait!* I didn't have a fireplace in my bedroom, and a tidal wave of memories crashed through me. Me heading into the woods for wolfsbane, the priestess replanting wolfsbane in our neighboring land, and wolves attacking me. Even Mr. No Pants popped in there, reminding me of his warning about the wolves at war, and how I'd gloriously gotten myself caught by a pack.

The earlier jitters swarmed through me, and I scrambled off a long table, my lower back stiff, hoping to avoid making a sound. Darn, the wolves had me lying there like a roast so they could just sit down and devour their dinner. I patted myself and glanced down. Yep, still wearing clothes, but they were dry now. How long had I been out?

A throbbing ache settled across my temple, and I rubbed the lump on my head from where the wolf had knocked me out.

The room lay barren of decorations. Wooden walls and more timber across the ceiling. The table in the middle, and a torn-up rug covered the hardwood in front of the fire; someone had scratched their claws on the frayed edges. No windows, just a closed door. And a strange musty and wet-dog-fur smell hung in the air.

My mind failed to make sense of where I was, and I couldn't formulate a thought. I turned on the spot, not recognizing anything. I froze, yet tingles pressed on my body to run, to put distance between me and the wolves. I choked on the breath from my lungs and tightness clasped my gut. *Time to leave.* I retreated toward the door, but my foot hit something. I flinched and looked down. I'd just bumped into a stack of logs for the fireplace. No sentimental objects sat on the mantelpiece behind me or paintings to indicate who owned the place. If there were photos of family, then maybe I'd stand a chance to plead to their softer side.

But I suspected this was a wolf shifter's home. Everything I'd heard about them painted them as savages who lived off the land and who followed their alpha to the death if he asked it of them. Except here I was in a house that had required someone to build it. Unless the shifters kidnapped humans to do their bidding? That notion sank through me like tar. What would they ask of me?

I rushed across the room, desperate to get out of this house.

But steps away from the door, it flung open, hitting the wall, and a flurry of cold air collided into me.

My heart struck my throat, and I staggered backward as a

man strode into the room. At first, my gaze bounced from his bare feet to his naked torso, then to the whole chiseled specimen standing before me. Why hadn't anyone told me shifters were gods in appearance? If I'd known, I may have stumbled into their territory before.

I glanced behind him, down a long corridor with wooden walls and several doors. This house was a lot larger than I had first thought. What was in the other rooms? Victims? Kidnapped humans?

My gaze fastened on the red material wrapped around the man's hips, worn as a skirt. So familiar. Near the bunched-up fabric at his side there was a small symbol of a black moon crest. Just like the one Grandma had sewn on her hooded cloak.

I scratched my neck, reaching for mine, but my cloak was gone. I scanned the room behind me. My bag sat in a corner alone. The wolves must have collected it after I'd dropped it in the woods. A sweet gesture, and so maybe not all hope was lost for me surviving the day.

I swung back around to the man dressed in part of *my* cloak. Fire hit my cheeks and I stormed closer, but he kicked the door shut, closing us inside together.

But right then I didn't care, not when an inferno burned me up from my toes to my head.

"How dare you?" I said, snatching the fabric off him. It unraveled at my touch. "You tore my cloak? How *could* you?" My eyes watered as I stared at the flowing red material in my hands. Hollowness spread throughout my chest, because I'd taken such good care of Grandma's garment and now to find it torn broke my heart. I barely held onto my sanity when she had passed, and each time I wore her cape, it felt as if she were with me.

"My grandmother gave me this," I hissed, wondering if I could sew it back onto the rest of the cloak, except it would never be the same. I wiped my cheeks and raised my chin, staring at the man's bangs, the color of cocoa, sweeping across his brow. Short hair edged along the sides of his head and the back. He studied me with softness in his eyes, as if pitying me. And only then did I realize the impact of me stripping him, and I burned for a whole different reason.

His girth down there had my knees quivering.

Okay, I'd had one boyfriend before, but he was normal-sized... Actually, in comparison, non-existent in the downstairs department.

The shifter laughed, his earlier stiff expression relaxed and unrestrained.

I lifted my gaze, convinced I'd turned into a berry in color. "What's going on? Why were you wearing my cloak and where am I? Where are your clothes?"

The man closed the distance between us, and I recoiled, gripping the fabric. Despite fear clouding my head, butterflies twirled in my stomach from imagining myself touching the muscled curves of his chest. He carried a beauty about him with his small nose and boyish charm. He wasn't built huge, but he had muscles and lots of them. His cheekbones brought out his glimmering eyes. The fire reflected in his pupils, flicking this way and that, changing the color from a gray to a grassy hue. If I'd crossed paths with him anywhere else, I'd have stopped in my tracks for a better look at the handsome man. Now I wasn't sure if I should run or try to talk him into turning me loose.

"You need not fear me," he said, his voice honeyed and low with a trace of huskiness. The complete opposite of what I'd expected.

"I beg to diff." I squared my shoulders to look bigger, though I couldn't achieve anywhere near the height of the stranger who towered over me. "Are you the shifter who rough handled me outside and head-butted me?"

The corner of his mouth lifted in an arrogant triumph, and he ran a hand through his short hair, drawing my attention to his flexing bicep.

"We prefer to call ourselves 'hunters.' 'Shifter' is such a *human* word, referring to anything that takes animal form."

"So you *were* the gray wolf?" My voice dipped.

"No, I'm not gray. That's Dagen."

I nodded, chewing on my cheek. *Dagen.* Must be the alpha? "So, what will you do with me? Can I leave?" Though the idea of returning home knotted my thoughts, thanks to the situation with the priestess. What was worse? Facing off against shifters... I mean 'hunters', or an angry leader? Not sure yet.

"Call me 'Nero.' And well,"—he licked his lips like a starved wolf who hadn't eaten for a week—"we have a slight problem."

"Hmm." I wasn't liking where this was going, and I didn't like being stuck in a house with Nero—and who knew where the other wolves lingered? Was their "slight problem" an inability to decide which one should tear me to shreds first? But Grandma had taught me to show no fear, because sometimes wearing confidence scared away the enemy. I tucked the part of her cloak into my back pocket.

I straightened my posture and approached the man, my sights on the door. "Well, good luck with your problem, and thanks for not eating me. But I must go."

Despite sweat dripping down my back, I kept my composure together and passed Nero. Every nerve crackled, and a shiver snaked down my spine. The door was in sight, and I reached for the handle.

Nero leaned a shoulder against the door, keeping it in place. He yawned as if this were a game... and what if it was?

I tugged on the doorknob with no luck.

"Little lamb, you're not going anywhere."

CHAPTER 4

"What's your name?" Nero asked, studying me from behind hooded eyes, his voice low and husky. Shadows leaped across his cheeks from the fireplace, masking his true expression.

But I wouldn't let him intimidate me with his charming ways, or by standing there in the nude. Didn't wolves wear clothes? And I'd heard enough tales to know when I ran from a wolf, it gave chase, so I stood my ground and responded, "Scarlet."

Maybe reasoning with him would save me from turning into his dinner. "You look like a kind man... Umm, I mean hunter. If you let me leave, I promise not to tell anyone about your secret den. And..." *Think*. What could I offer a wolf shifter who stared at me as if I were his meal? "Herbs. I'm an expert at healing and..." I twisted around to find my bag and darted toward it.

With the satchel tucked under an arm, I dug inside, as I had all my herbs packed in separate little pouches. But water soaked everything, and prickly herbs stuck to my fingertips, meaning something had opened, maybe even been ruined.

Coldness wrapped around my chest at the thought that I had nothing to offer him. But I had no other option, and Nero wouldn't know the difference. I just had to escape. Part of me toyed with the idea of tossing wolfsbane into his face, but I wasn't ready to take on a wolf, now or ever. First, I had to try to negotiate, so I showed him my small medicine bag I carried everywhere. Grandma had always taught me to be prepared. Guess she'd never believed I'd be in a wolf's den, though.

Water droplets fell to the wooden floor, causing Nero to arch an eyebrow.

"It's just water." I choked out a laugh. "But the herbs are great to make a healing tea or rub them on a wound to stop infection."

When he didn't respond, I dove back into the bag, well aware that I had a batch of jimsonweed. The stuff was hard to come by and only grew high on the mountains where the bears lived. My fingers caressed the silky fabric, and I presented it to Nero, who tilted his head, studying the offering. Was he interested? That gave me hope.

"Mix this into someone's drink and they will hallucinate for a short while," I explained.

His nose wrinkled. "Why would a little lamb like you be carrying such a potion?"

I swallowed the thickness rubbing my throat. "Grandma always told me to carry a small amount should someone ever kidnap me."

He smirked.

Every inch of me tingled to recoil, but I refused to show him fear.

Nero didn't respond, and the jitters returned to my stomach. Had I said too much and now he saw me as a threat?

"Listen," he started and reached for my wrist, but the moment his fingers grazed mine, a spark zipped up my arm. I flinched back, and his head shot up, his eyes widening.

"What was that?" he asked.

I shook my head because I'd never felt anything like that before—when I wasn't amplifying plants, anyhow. The tiny spark now swirled in the pit of my gut, coiling in on itself. "As much as I'm enjoying your company, I think it's time for me to leave."

He stared at me for the longest moment, but his stoic expression gave nothing away, and I clutched my wet bag to my chest, regretting it at once as the water soaked through my top, freezing my skin. The moment I lowered it, Nero's gaze dipped, and I followed his gaze to my hardened nipples pressing against the fabric plastered to my body. My cheeks burned, and I caught the slight twitch of his hardness. Oh, crap... If he got aroused that quickly, had I been wrong about his intentions this whole time?

Nero laughed, the sound powerful and crashing through me like torrential rain. He leaned in closer, his lips so close to mine, I could feel them on my skin. I didn't back away, so hooray for me, though my legs wobbled. My palms tingled with the desire to reach out and see if his muscles were as hard as they looked. It was utter madness. I wasn't supposed to get hot and bothered by my enemy, but he fogged my mind.

Wolves had killed my parents, and I should have shoved the jimsonweed into Nero's face, but Grandma's words about my parents' deaths kept resurfacing. *Not everything in life is as straightforward as it seems. There are secrets everywhere.* Nero appeared to be only a few years older than me, so he wouldn't have had anything to do with their deaths. But a wolf was a wolf, known for their aggressiveness, their territorial ways, their suspicion of strangers. I had no reason to believe that his kind didn't take my parents. I might have been next. With the way Nero was observing me, I ought to have run for my life. Yet a strange sensation teased me with the possibility of him wishing for more than a taste of my blood. Beyond all my rationale, I yearned to discover what he indeed wanted from me.

"I'm not going to hurt you. We just saved you from the other wolf." Nero's voice shattered through my thoughts like glass, bringing me back to the present.

A desperate, suffocating urge tightened around my lungs as I inhaled his musk and timber scent. I lost my mind to his gray wolf-eyes, and butterflies swarmed my stomach like the time Timmy had asked me on my first date. Except this was a hundred times stronger. It was too much but not enough at the same time.

Catching my breath, I asked, "C-Can I go home now?"

He raised a hand and shifted a loose strand of hair caught on my lashes. He threaded his fingers to the back of my head and grabbed my hair in his fist, tilting my chin up with his other hand, our gazes meeting. Panic should have rattled me at the core, and I shouldn't have allowed this, but flames circled my libido. I'd never liked dominant men... but Nero was doing something to me I couldn't get enough of. It was wrong, and my emotions battled back and forth.

His warm exhale danced across my face and his mouth grazed mine. My knees buckled under me as his fiery passion engulfed me.

Except, what was I doing? What were his intentions? Every fiber of my being demanded I give myself to this stranger, but instead, I shoved my hands into his chest and drove him backward.

I gasped for air and stared at the glazed expression crawling over his face. "I'm not someone you can take advantage of."

His shoulders rolled forward. "Can't you feel it?" he growled.

I slid farther away along the wall, certain I'd fallen down a hole because my emotions weren't making sense. I shouldn't feel anything but anger toward this shifter. And why weren't there any windows in this room?

"The intensity of our connection," he continued. "I've never felt this before."

"What I feel is confusion." Sure, if I continued, I was convinced my panties might have melted off, but that didn't make it right. "Who exactly are you? And where are we?"

We exchanged glances, unblinking. He was a hunter and ate my kind... Heavens, how I'd love for him to devour me. The image of him between my thighs, licking me, had me shuddering. *Stop it!*

A guttural growl echoed throughout the house, and I choked at the sound.

Nero smiled at me as if he knew something I didn't. "We better go," he declared, as if he hadn't just kissed me.

I took a breath before asking, "What was that?"

He broke away, and a chill found me. The moment he opened the door, a rush of cool air brushed past. I couldn't move when my thoughts stayed with what danger lay out there.

Slumped against the wall, I couldn't get enough air into my lungs. I could barely move, let alone attempt walking.

"Little lamb, the time has come to meet Dagen and for you to help us with our problem." He stretched out an arm, his palm upward, his fingers extended toward me.

At first, I couldn't find my voice. Confusion tore at my mind, from the threat prickling down my spine. I'd heard tales of people getting kidnapped by wolves. And meeting with this Dagen had me shaking as I recalled the way he had stared at me in the woods while in his wolf form. Dagen had to be the alpha in charge. But in any case, it wasn't as if I knew a way out of this house, so I'd play along until I found an escape, then I'd do what it took to get out. Though I kept wondering what in the world he'd done to make me fall over myself to kiss him.

I picked up the dropped herbs, stuffed them into the bag, and stepped forward, refusing his hand. The man towered over me, bigger than anyone I'd ever encountered, but I refused to let him intimidate me.

Nero guided me down the dark hallway with doors and now windows, the tapping of our footsteps on floorboards sounding around us. "Where are we?" I asked.

We took a sharp left at the end before he pushed open a door that had a ragged hole in the bottom paneling as if someone had kicked it.

Unease hurt my stomach, and each inhale grew shorter, faster.

"This is one of Oryn's places," Nero explained, as if I should know who that was.

Was Oryn the black wolf?

Nero lead me into a bedroom illuminated by a single, short candle on a bedside table. In the middle of the room sat a bed with a man lying on his back, covered by a woolen blanket that reached his waist. The room smelled sickly sweet of wet dog fur. Shadows shrouded the corners, and again, there were no windows. What was the deal with that? Nero approached the bed and placed a palm to the man's forehead.

"Is he sick?" I closed the distance, my boots clip-clopping against the wooden floorboards, when a growl echoed from my right.

I flinched, my pulse jolting into hyper mode, just as a blur rushed me from the shadows.

A cry fell from my throat, and I stumbled backward as

something huge, black, and fast barreled into me. My feet tangled, and I fell over, hitting the floor. A wolf's snout hovered inches over my face, lips peeled back, fangs on display. Hot breath streamed over me. The guttural sound of death churned through his chest.

I yelled as the animal straddled me, my arms across my face, expecting my throat to be torn out.

"Oryn, back off." Nero's voice boomed.

He pressed a foot against the wolf's rump, shoving him aside. "Now!" he roared.

Nothing made me want to meet Oryn, if this was the welcoming he offered. He was the type of wolf that those terrifying shifter horror stories were based on.

With a final snarl, Oryn leaped off me and paced around the bed, grumbling to himself.

Was he angry because I was in his home? I'd gladly leave if that was the case. I didn't want to be here when I'd rather return home and ensure my store wasn't being torn down by the priestess and Santos remained safe. For too long, I'd survived by not drawing attention to myself, now... I'd gone and done that royally.

Nero grabbed my forearm and wrenched me to my feet so fast, I bumped into his side. "It's all right, little lamb. Don't pay Oryn any mind. He's in a pissy mood."

I met the wolf's gaze from across the bed. He didn't move, but he watched me. He'd eat me if he got the chance. I felt it in my bones.

Dread sat in my chest, eroding the last threads of confidence I held on to. I sidled up against Nero, his warmth driving away the terror clenching to my ribs.

Oryn huffed and darted from the room, his nails scratching the floorboards.

"What's wrong with him?" I asked.

"Oryn is a great hunter, and he doesn't let many get close to him."

Latter part was relatable. "When my grandma passed, I didn't talk to anyone for weeks and wanted to hide from the world. Did he lose someone close to him?"

Nero shook his head. "Now, about our little issue."

Okay, a sensitive topic of conversation. I glanced down at the man in bed, who resembled a statue of a god with honey-colored hair that reached his shoulders. Flawless skin, even if pale and sweaty, a broad jawline and a strong nose that looked as if it had been broken before. A scar lined his temple and hairline. Healed claw marks ran down his neck and across his chest. What had happened in his life to gain such wounds? I moved to the other side of the bed to better study the shifter I assumed was Dagen. I reached over and ran a finger across a bumpy scar lining his collarbone. "Who did this to him?"

"Bears, humans, wolves," Nero said, folding his arms across his chest, and yet my attention fell to his amazing package, bringing the heat back to my face.

"Here, put this back on." I handed him the piece of red cloak tucked into the back of my pants. "You've torn it already."

"The fabric was ripped when we took it off you." He accepted the piece, then wrapped it around himself. His hardness hadn't fully gone down and the curved form pressed through the material. Heavens, I ought to have been used to this, since nude men always seemed to turn up on my doorstep, and Bee talked about men all the time, but Nero affected me like no other.

I returned my attention to the hunter on the mattress. My heart ached at seeing someone covered in so many scars. How many battles had he fought? "Why did everyone attack him?"

"Dagen's an alpha. He must defend his territory from invaders, other wolves who don't follow his command, or who challenge his position. Otherwise, he'll die."

"Shit." The tales of aggressive hunters were real. I pitied him. "And you're Dagen's beta?"

Nero squared his shoulders and puffed out his cheeks. "Little lamb, Oryn, Dagen, and I are all alphas. Our land was split into three territories centuries ago, and we each rule a jurisdiction, as our predecessors had."

I scratched my head. "Then why are you all three together?" Mr. No Pants had said the wolves were at war. Was it because there were three bosses? "I spoke to a man who traveled through your land this morning. He lost his pants to a wolf attack, which I guess is inconsequential, but he said there was a war brewing between wolves. Is that true?"

Nero sighed and ran a hand through his hair. "Oh, I remember the bastard, and he was lucky I only ripped off his pants, not his legs. He crossed our land from Darkwoods to reach Terra without approval to enter our territory. But yes, we are having wolf issues at the moment, but that's our problem to solve." He paused. "Your concern is helping us cure Dagen."

"What's wrong with him?" I placed a hand on his brow. He was burning up.

"I was hoping you could tell us. Whatever you sprayed on him has affected him. We need your help to make him wake up."

The reason I had created my potions was to deter animals, never to hurt them. "I didn't mean to harm him. I thought you were going to kill me, but the spray is only a deterrent." Heavens, what had I done? I didn't even know these hunters, but when I looked into Nero's eyes, a softness filled them, reassuring me. "I'm sorry."

Now I understood Oryn's reaction and why he'd attacked

me. He blamed me for Dagen's state. But, in all fairness, they'd terrified me in the woods. Then I remembered the wolfsbane that had spilled into my bag and caught on the citrus spritzer. Had that tainted the potion? *Oh, mother of pearl!*

I had inadvertently injured Dagen. Yet every time I looked at Nero, I pictured his lips all over my body. And him staring at me like a starved sex-god wasn't helping. A distraction was in order. This was enemy land, and I was in danger. That meant focusing, watching, and listening for the right moment to make my move and escape.

"So, if I help your friend, you'll let me go, right?" If Dagen died, what would stop them from exacting revenge on me?

Nero headed out of the room. "Holler if you need me." His voice grew dark and distant.

"Can you bring me a bucket of boiling water and bandages?" I called out, not ready to deal with emotions I didn't understand.

I should have been planning my escape to get out of wolf territory, but then why did it feel as if a blade twisted in my gut at the thought of leaving this wolf shifter unconscious from my potion?

CHAPTER 5

"Well, looks like it's just you and me," I said to Dagen, who remained unconscious on the bed after the others had left. "I help you and hopefully that buys me my freedom, right? Only fair. I mean, I did put you in that bed accidentally when you attacked me. But Nero said you were saving me from the wolf, and for that I owe you." Huffing, I dropped my bag on the mattress and rummaged through the contents, remembering I had tossed the bottle at Dagen in the woods. "Nothing in the potion should have harmed you."

I never used toxic ingredients. But wolfsbane root had tangled with the bottle, so that meant it must have somehow tainted the potion and I might have inadvertently poisoned him. Wolfsbane was toxic to wolves. If ingested, it killed them quickly. Back in ancient times, before Haven was split into seven territories, all races lived together, and they fought endlessly. The stories explained that human guards would tip arrows with wolfsbane to hunt animals and keep savage wolves at bay.

So the urgency to fix Dagen sat on my chest. I had no idea

what had made him sick, and what if the wolfsbane was slowly killing him? If he hadn't died yet, there was hope he hadn't swallowed any of the spritz. Oryn was ready to rip my head off already, so what would he do if his friend passed because of my mistake? A shiver gripped me, because I didn't want to find out.

Okay, I have to fix this and fast.

Nero returned carrying a bucket of steaming water, which he placed near the end of the bed, along with several strips of fabric for bandages.

"I'm thinking he has wolfsbane poisoning," I explained. "So I need—"

"Wait!" Nero's deep voice sliced through mine. "Why would he be poisoned, when that plant doesn't grow in the Den?"

I swallowed past the thickness in my throat, hating how I cringed on the inside, loathing how Nero stared at me as if I were a monster. My words raced. "There's wolfsbane in my bag. I collected it for a friend back in Terra. But the roots got caught on my protection spray. Traces of it must have hit Dagen's face when I splashed him. I'm so sorry. But he's not dead, so it's not too late."

Nero said nothing but clenched and unclenched his hands, his attention on Dagen, and my chest constricted.

"Look, I'll do everything to help him. I'm an herbalist healer. But I require a few more things. Vinegar, salt, and more fabric."

Nero wasn't responding, so I closed the distance and touched his arm, and that buzz zapped through. He looked down at his hand, then raised his chin and sniffed the air.

"I can smell your scent and a damp, mossy odor from your bag, but I didn't pick up the wolfsbane earlier." The harsh tone behind his words had me backing away.

I nodded. "It's loose in my bag and probably wet from the river."

His face paled. "Hand over everything."

"But I've got my other herbs in there, too." I picked up the bag from where I'd dropped it, squaring my shoulders.

Nero snatched the handle from my hands and stormed out of the room. A swirl of darkness consumed my thoughts. What was he going to do? Burn my belongings? But worrying about what I couldn't control wouldn't keep me alive. So I dragged the bucket to the side of the bed and drenched a piece of fabric in the steaming hot water, the scorching heat pinching my skin.

I had to heal Dagen and prove to Nero I wasn't a threat, then he'd have to release me, though part of me still craved Nero. I curled the blanket down to Dagen's ankles and found him naked. *Of course.* Even unconscious, he was huge. What was up with shifters? All I could say was that she wolves were a lucky set of ladies.

Picking up a wet bandage, I squeezed out the water, my hands burning, but it was essential the bandages remained hot against his limbs. "Just so you know," I said to Dagen, "you will not disappoint whoever your future mate is. Or your current mate. You must have a harem of girls." I continued covering his legs with the hot strips of material. The next piece would need two layers to sit across his strong thigh.

I hurried, but when my hand nudged his privates, he twitched.

Nero returned, and I froze, hands flinched to my chest, my stomach locked tight. "Everything is fine."

His nose wrinkled. "Is Dagen awake?"

Dagen had twitched at my touch, which was a fantastic reaction because it meant his body wasn't numb. But I couldn't bring myself tell Nero that I touched his friend's privates. *Nope.*

I rushed to the bucket and prepared another bandage. Nero set a wooden container with what smelled like vinegar near the bed along with a bag of salt and dumped a mountain of material strips the color of hide on the floor. Had the shifters stolen them from someone in Terra?

"Do all shifters get a lot of injuries?" I asked. In haste, I covered Dagen's other leg, refusing to put my hand anywhere near his... privates.

"This is Oryn's house, and he uses the place as a resting home for wolves in the vicinity."

With the blanket rolled back up Dagen's legs, I tucked him in tight. Heat radiated from him, which was perfect. "So it's also a medical house, then?"

Grandma had always wanted to expand the herbal store into a healing place for people to stay for a few nights, treating their ailments. She insisted everyone deserved help. So whether they were shifters or not, I wouldn't discriminate and help Dagen as best as I could.

"Guess so." Nero's words snapped me back to reality. He leaned a shoulder into the frame of the doorway, and I sensed him watching me. What was he thinking? How helpful I was, or how he'd hunt me down when I finished?

Before long, I had Dagen's arms covered in moist fabric. I dumped the salt into the vinegar and stirred with my hand. I dunked a larger piece of fabric inside.

"What are you doing?" Nero asked.

I patted the cold material across Dagen's chest, covering him from his bellybutton to his neck. "Wolfsbane attacks major organs while numbing limbs. So I need to bring warmth to his extremities so they get feeling back. I use the salt in vinegar to extract any poisons in his torso." I ran another damp strip across Dagen's brow and down his face, wiping away the perspiration. What I needed was for him to drink some vinegar so he could vomit more of the poison out.

Nero had left again. Okay, back to alone time with Mr. Handsome. Fine with me. "More time for us to chat," I said and continued wiping a cold rag across his closed eyes and dried lips, hoping it would help awaken him.

Back in the woods, I hadn't recalled seeing any herbs that could assist him, but then again, I'd spent my time trying to survive. So why was that first wolf I encountered so vicious and blood-hungry while Nero remained calm? Well, okay, Oryn seemed crazed, and he freaked me out. Must be a wolf thing and I didn't get it. If this was the hospitality they dished out, it made sense why no one dared enter their territory. Still, hanging out in their house wasn't conducive to ensuring I survived another day. I was their prisoner. The fact that they hadn't killed me yet didn't mean it wasn't a matter of time.

Yet my thoughts swirled back to Nero's kiss, and the craziness of me craving him. What was that about? I must have drunk too much river water, and it had made me delusional. Plus, a charge of electricity had shuddered through me back in the stream. Had that been in my mind too?

I wiped Dagen's brow once more. "You not waking up might be the only thing keeping me alive. How ironic." In any other situation, I might have hollered with laughter.

An explosive growl boomed throughout the house, and I shuddered, my back plastered to the wall near the bed.

I glanced into the dark corridor. What was that sound and where did the other doors lead? Wiping my wet hands down my pants, I crept toward the corridor. Darkness consumed the hallway, but farther to my left lay a door. I pushed one leg forward, then the other, my gaze fixed on the point where the hall turned. I kept expecting Oryn to come charging in and rip into me, but I had to know where I was.

Okay, keep it together. Once I get out, I run. I'd navigate home by finding a way back up the cliff I'd fallen from.

With quick steps, I reached the first door and touched the brass knob. Every inch of me trembled as I twisted the handle. I held my breath as I entered a pitch-black room. With the light behind me shining inside, I found three piles of blankets stacked against the wall. Nothing else. Were these their sleeping quarters? Squinting, I stared through the dark. Zilch. Along with no windows.

Dead end.

A sinking feeling rattled through me, so I continued down the hallway, determined to find the way out. My gaze swung left and right in the hall, but nothing came for me.

More sounds, like a dying animal screeching. My skin pinpricked, and more than anything I wanted to help the poor thing. Were they torturing their meal? I was in a wolf's home. But Nero explained this was more of a medical house, so maybe a shifter lay hurt? I inched down the hallway and around the corner to find several other doorways, along with the one at the end. Exactly where I'd woken up on the table in front of a fireplace.

The next one I checked turned out to be a closet, stacked with towels, striped fabric, and even a pillow. That part made me smirk as I pictured a tough wolf needing a pillow, but I supposed everyone needed comfort. It had taken me months to find the right filling for my pillow back home as I woke up day after day with the sorest neck and a headache.

I opened the next door. Golden light flooded out, stealing the darkness from the hallway.

"Come in, Scarlet," Nero said.

My heart thumped beneath my breastbone as too many scenarios filled my mind. Him turning all furry on me for trying to escape, or maybe I'd stumbled across him gorging on a victim. Or he was sharpening his teeth and prepared to chain me up. *Heavens.*

But doing nothing wasn't an option, so I stepped into a large kitchen lit by a fireplace, with a cauldron suspended over the flames. The most delicious soup aroma filled my nostrils.

Across from the mantel was a long table, where Nero lounged in a chair, his legs propped up on an empty seat and crossed at the ankles. Naked, no longer wearing my cloak to cover himself. "I was wondering how long it would take you to explore."

Think fast. The first thing that popped into my head came streaming out. "Well, I need more herbs to help your friend. And where's my bag?"

"Your bag is in a safe place for now. I can't risk having wolfsbane around the house."

I scanned the room, noting the stool near the fireplace was stacked with a handful of plates and bowls. Okay, maybe they weren't complete savages. But when my gaze settled on the door at the rear of the room, a sprinkle of hope spiked my adrenaline. Was that the way outside?

"It's locked for your own safety," Nero said. "Why don't you take a seat? I'll get you some food."

"Oh no, I'm okay. I prefer you tell me what's going on here. Am I in danger? Why are three alphas living together when you said earlier you had your own packs?"

The earlier growl of a hurt animal boomed again, and I flinched, then hurried to a chair, closer to Nero. I glanced toward the hallway. "What *is* that?"

He sighed and was on his feet, naked, and, as much as I tried to resist, my attention dipped to his abundant package. Gosh, I'd never seen so much male flesh in my life, ever. I pictured Bee flashing me two thumbs up for my effort. How can he be perfect in every way, yet terrifying?

"It's Oryn." Nero collected a bowl and filled it with the contents from the cauldron.

"What's wrong with him?" I tucked a leg underneath me on the seat, studying the walls for keys and a way out. Instead, I only saw dried herbs hanging off a hook. Sage, oregano, and thyme.

"He's trying to find himself right now, and we're here to sort out a few problems. It's our meeting point." Nero placed the bowl in front of me. No spoon.

"Root vegetable soup." He sat on a seat next to me. "It's packed with herbs and I was thinking once Dagen woke up, it would help him."

I stared at the meal, its steam curling upward and the smell enticing my gut to growl with hunger. But my mind stayed on Nero's words and how caring he was to make a soup for his friend. I didn't know a single man back home who knew how to cook. Despite his flirtatious attitude, Nero had a huge heart. Would that mean he wouldn't harm me? He didn't seem like a murderer, but, then again, I'd never encountered one before.

"There's no poison or anything in there," he continued. "If I wanted to take you out, I'd use my teeth." He winked and while his words should have scared me, his sexy gesture had my gaze dipping to his luscious lips, the dip in his throat, and down to his bare chest.

My gut ached and food sounded amazing. I lifted the bowl to my lips and took a sip. Savory, tangy, and appetizing. Not too hot either, so I gulped down several mouthfuls, chewing on what tasted like spinach. I wiped my mouth and glanced up at Nero, who studied me with a look of curiosity. Had he never seen anyone enjoy their food before?

"Delicious?" he asked.

"Divine, and the lemon is subtle but lingers on my tongue." I swallowed another mouthful, the heat racing through me. "Maybe not as good as my recipe, but close." I smirked, and Nero laughed, the sound joyful and loud.

"If I had access to more ingredients, I'd make you pork jambalaya, a pot recipe I got from a traveler I once met from the Tritonia realm. You'd be on your third bowl by now." The corners of his mouth lifted with a confident grin.

My knees bounced. "I've tried it with chicken, loved it, and tried remaking it. Not sure I did it justice, but I need to keep experimenting." I used to cook most nights Grandma while she ground fresh leaves into pastes for healing different sicknesses. I had told her often I wanted to offer dishes at the store that helped ill people. Grandma said I inherited my passion for cooking from my mother.

Nero nodded. "I like that you pay attention to your food. Too many people don't care or even experiment with flavors enough."

Finishing my dish, I pushed it away. "So how come you, an alpha, are into cooking?"

Nero was on his feet and collected my empty bowl. "My mother brought me up on her own and when she fell ill, I had two younger, fussy brothers who refused to eat anything, so I had no choice but to get creative. And it turns out, I enjoyed making meals. Now I hold regular classes with my pack." His eyes brightened, and he revealed perfectly aligned teeth, his smile a ray of sunshine. It did something to me. It drove away my earlier worries, and for those few moments, I felt as if I were chatting with Bee.

Nero warmed his hands near the fire, watching me, and just having his eyes lingering on me sent a tingle up my thighs. I lowered my gaze, confused by my strange attraction to Nero. I could picture myself chatting with him for days about foods we enjoyed, both of us trying different dishes at the markets. He had that easy approachable feel about him, which I never would have expected from a shifter.

"How's Dagen doing?" he asked. "When will he wake?"

"I've never healed a shifter... I mean a hunter. I'm trying what I would do to an afflicted person."

He spoke with his back to me. "So, what were you doing in the Den? How did you get here?"

"Funny story." I broke into a quick rendition, including why I'd collected the wolfsbane, the priestess' threat, and how I'd almost drowned. "It was an accident. I'd been running for my life."

"I've heard rumors your leader has ordered the slaughter of any wolves her guards cross paths with. I don't order my pack to kill innocents." He closed the distance between us and sagged into his seat. "Why don't you overthrow her? Someone should challenge her and take the spot."

I twisted to face him. "It doesn't work that way in Terra. She's part royalty, so she inherited the role. The only person to take over would be another member of her family. Her younger sister maybe." I shrugged.

"Makes little sense to keep someone like that in power."

We sat there, and, instead of awkwardness, a calm settled into my muscles, a newfound confidence fueling my question. "Am I your prisoner?"

He tilted his head to the side. "Would that make you feel more comfortable?"

I slouched in my seat. "That doesn't even make sense."

"Well, by believing you're in danger, then your focus is simple: escaping at any cost." He ran a hand across his mouth, drawing my attention to his parted lips, making me remember their softness against me. "But what if you wanted to stay of your own volition?"

I folded my arms. "Seems unlikely."

Nero moved toward me so fast, I stiffened. His piercing

gray wolf-eyes locked on to me with hunger. "I still feel that magnetic pull toward you, and I don't understand why."

Urgency poured through me, the kind that said *get out of there*. I slid out of my chair and backed up against a wall. A strange sensation engulfed me, trepidation blended with excitement. I couldn't understand my emotions.

He advanced and pinned me between him and the wall, a hand pressed above my shoulder. "Little lamb." He trailed his fingers down my arm, and a spark of energy zapped between us. "What have you done to me?"

I shivered from his feathery touch, unable to find my voice. I ought to have pushed him away, reminded him if I wasn't a prisoner, why didn't they show me the way out? Except the back of my mind spawned doubts as I imagined myself with him. And yes, I felt the unyielding attraction for Nero... no, it was more than that... a temptation I couldn't ignore. What was wrong with me?

"When I carried you into the house to keep you protected, my wolf responded to you, craved you. Even now, he's demanding I take you, claim you for eternity."

"B-But I'm not a wolf." I should have laughed at my response, yet I hung on to his words. To have someone as gorgeous and dangerous as Nero claim he wanted me did things to my rational thinking. Maybe I had to get out and date more, except what he'd said earlier about feeling a connection hammered through me. In his presence, I lost all logical thoughts, and his touches gave me physical jolts. I should have screamed and run in the opposite direction.

"I can't explain it, either. Everything about you draws me to you," he whispered in my ear. "Your scent, your voice, your response to my demands all rile up my wolf."

A moan escaped from my throat. Confusion, heated emotions, and decisions whirled on my mind. Despite every-thing, being this close to Nero had the doubts cascading into the background. "I feel it, too," I mumbled. "I can't think when I'm around you. But I can't stay here. My home is in danger, as is my assistant at my herbal store. And wolves will kill me if I remain in the Den. I need to leave, please."

A low growl rumbled deep through Nero's chest, and he pulled away, leaving me breathless.

"I don't know what's wrong with me?" He grumbled as his gaze lowered, his brow marring into a dozen lines. "Around you, it's like my wolf takes over and insists on taking you."

I had no words because I'd never felt this drawn to anyone before. And there were a couple of potential boyfriends in town I fantasized about, but that was nothing compared to the heat burning me at the core for Nero. My breaths sped in his presence. And something deep inside me coiled so tight, I feared my heart my stop beating if I didn't take Nero. And just thinking those words had me feeling like an idiot. I definitely must have hit my head, but what about Nero? Why was he feeling the same way?

No way in the world would a man who looked like him be interested in me. Let alone a shifter.

When he lifted his gaze, I took shaky, shallow breaths, unable to move. Something was happening between us... something dark, terrifying, and exciting. And too fast, because I never fell for anyone this quick. Thoughts fluttered out of my mind, replaced with pure adrenaline and desire. A niggling fear swirled in my chest that I'd made a mistake playing with the devil.

The conflict flashed across his face, and he blinked too fast, his hands curling into fists. He gasped for air. His eyes studied me as a predator might do, except this was different. Under his gaze, I melted into a puddle, and a sense of comfort flooded me as if we'd be in this position dozens of times. And resisting each other seemed foolish.

With one quick step, he pulled me against his chest and kissed me. Tingles exploded from where our lips touched, spreading through the rest of my body. The intoxicating scent of his muskiness engulfed me. His tongue pressed the seam of my mouth, and my world fell away as I parted my lips. Smoldering heat burned deep inside. A surge of power bubbled beneath the surface, ready to explode.

CHAPTER 6

*N*ero licked my neck, and a mewl rolled past my throat. It was impossible to resist the shifter who had only existed in my dreams before today, but now he promised me heaven, and there was no going back. I had jumped onboard and was already taking charge.

I combed my fingers through his hair, pulling him closer. His hands wormed their way up my shirt, finding flesh. His electric touch left me tingling, begging for more. Where had this man been my whole life?

He towered over me, wearing a devilish grin, and tugged my vest and top over my head. The coldness washed across my breasts, my skin prickling with need.

I shivered, and he reached over, his hands scooping under my breasts, kneading them, his thumbs flicking my nipples. They tightened and hurt in the most exhilarating way. I wasn't sure if anyone had ever exploded from being turned on too much, but I might be the first. The apex of my legs burned like a volcano about to burst.

"Mine." His voice deepened.

"Hmm." I moaned.

He kneeled in front, capturing a nipple into his mouth, and my knees wobbled. His wet tongue flicked me fast, suckling on me. My insides trembled with the desperation to have Nero fill me.

"Little lamb, I will devour you and you'll beg for more."

I scanned my mind for a smartass response, but instead, a gasp escaped. Great, nothing there but a horny-induced brain.

Nero laughed, loud and thick, and the sparkle in his eyes made me believe he genuinely loved my answer. A trickle of excitement zipped down to the pit of my stomach, rocking me on the spot.

"Is that a threat or a promise?" I purred, having found my voice.

"Ha, I adore when you let yourself go." His fingers flipped open the buttons of my pants and dragged them and my underwear down my legs so fast, I almost lost my footing, but he held on to my hips, steadying me.

So I stepped out of my clothes, standing naked next to a hunk who was also nude. I chewed on my cheek.

"Something about you calls to my wolf," he began. "No one's ever done that. And I know you can sense it, too." He drew me closer, his warmth radiating across my body, his erection nestled against my stomach. "But I have one problem..." He chuckled. "Well, actually, I've got plenty, but right now, only one comes to mind."

"A-And that is?" I held on to his thick arms as if they were tree trunks. Was he pushing me away after seeing how easy I was, and now he'd mock me and leave? Or was it he only wanted one thing from me... as insane as it sounded, I'd be fine were the latter his choice. An insatiable itch gripped my libido and unless I scratched it, I'd go mad. And who would know if I caved to a god of a wolf shifter...? Only I would. I'd carry those memories with me for eternity. It might ruin me for any other man, but if I did nothing, I'd kick myself. Damn, if I told Bee, she'd never let me hear the end of it if I didn't let Nero take me.

I glanced up at Nero, adoring how he stared at me as if I were a slice of honeyed cake.

"Once I fuck you, I'm not sure I could ever leave you." He ran a hand across my chin and his thumb rested on my lower lip. "In hunter tradition, once a wolf claims someone, they're together for life."

His admittance rocked through me. Sure, I was ready for a fun day of humping Nero, but now he was talking about mating. A life event. I wasn't a shifter, so his rules wouldn't apply to me, right?

He cupped my face and kissed me. "Are you sure you want to do this, little lamb?" he asked.

I licked my lips. "So, this mating thing only happens when two people have…"

"Sex. But not just any couple joining… My inner wolf needs to have made a connection."

As much as my logical mind tried to push forward and make sense of the situation, it was my horny-starved body that took over, thrumming with urgency. "I'm not from your world and I'm not a wolf, but it is weird that I feel as if we belong together. Like, if you left me, I'd forget how to breathe. I don't understand the mating thing or how it applies here, but for now, I want you. To have you keep your promise and forget the constant dread that has made its home in my heart. I'm tired of being scared and confused. But this"—I placed a palm to my chest and then his —"feels real."

He pressed my knuckles to his lips while his other hand cupped my butt. "I can't walk away from this moment either."

I lifted myself on tippy toes and grazed his mouth with mine. He returned the favor twofold, hungry and savage. Just this once, I yearned to follow my gut instinct, and the confirmation bellowed in my skull. "I give myself to you," I purred.

His kisses intensified. He pressed me up against the wall, his hands roaming across my naked body. *Need* was such a small word, but right now it shuddered through my body.

Nero's fingers slid to my waist, and he lifted me off my feet as if I weighed nothing. "Wrap those sexy legs around my neck and grab on to the rafter over your head."

My heart raced as he lifted me higher above him. "What?" Nervous as hell, I was so turned on at having his face cocooned between my thighs. I grasped the wooden beam running across the ceiling.

"I've got you, little lamb." He gripped my ass.

I could barely catch my breath as I hovered so high in the room, not sure how I felt about his acrobatic act. Was this how wolves did it? But the moment his lips clasped my clit, I convulsed.

"Oh, h-hell, Nero."

He gave an approving sound and flicked his tongue. I drifted on the clouds, lost, and consumed by the arousal owning me. His thumb thrummed against my clit, slowly, drawing out the orgasm rushing forward. His tongue penetrated me.

"Nero. Nero…" My entire body convulsed from pleasure. I belonged to him wholly.

I screamed, unable to hold back the intensity, the ecstasy. And Nero wasn't letting go but was sucking every drop. My privates throbbed, and he licked my entrance, consuming me. I wriggled, every muscle aching.

"That was incredible." I labored the words.

"It's only the beginning." With his touch sliding to my waist, he shouldered one of my legs off him, followed by the other. "Let go, I've got you."

And I did let go, as if all doubts and worries had escaped

me. I slid down, our bodies rubbing against one another, and he held me until my feet reached the floor. Then he pulled me closer, face to face. "Your taste is intoxicating." He pulled my legs over his hips, and the tip of his hardness caressed my entrance. "I'm going to fuck you now, little lamb."

"Heavens, yes. Please, I can't wait too much longer." I didn't care who heard my screams because I had to have Nero inside me.

He laughed again, the sound stroking the length of my spine, leaving me wet with anticipation. I gripped his shoulders as he pushed into me. I groaned as his thickness widened me, consumed me.

He thrust faster, and I screamed. It hurt and I loved it. I rocked my hips, but he'd already pulled out and back in, slow at first, as if testing me.

His gaze never left mine, and his eyes drowned in elation.

With each quickened slam, I gasped for air. His slaps grew faster, harder, and I mewled for more. "Yes!"

I met each strike, needing him deeper, soaked beneath his passion. Unrelenting, he pounded into me, never easing, and I drowned beneath his desire, unsure where I started and he ended.

"Scream for me, little lamb," he demanded.

And, as if my body listened to his command, the sound flew past my throat, and the sensation tipped me over the edge. A second orgasm gripped me. I quivered, unable to stop, my eyes clasped tight as I let myself go, unable to believe such pleasure was even possible. I ached to remain on this high forever.

My walls clenched, squeezing him. Our bodies grew sweaty and scorching hot. He groaned with his own pleasure, pulsing within me.

I opened my eyes, smiling, but movement in the hallway

drew my attention , and there stood Oryn in his black wolf form, staring at us, his lips curled over teeth.

"Shit!" I said, but Nero didn't let go.

"Ignore him. He's not himself at the moment."

So many questions swirled in my thoughts, yet with Nero still buried deep within and a wolf staring on, my emotions tangled into a knot between hiding and begging Nero for more. At the same time, a sense of heightened energy poured through my veins, buzzing through me, leaving me ready to take on the world.

With a growl, the wolf retreated into the darkened hall and vanished.

"What's his problem?" I asked.

Nero slid out of me before placing me on my feet. He planted a kiss on my head. "Oryn is facing challenges, and I'm giving him space."

What did that mean? But after that most incredible experience, I was more worried I'd never see Nero again once I returned home. A sting settled beneath my breastbone. I stared down and noticed a white line of energy skipping over the tips of my fingers.

"How are you doing that?" Nero asked, glancing down, but he tightened his arms around me, and I adored his protectiveness more than I imagined possible.

I refocused on my hand. "I've always had this ability to empower herbs with a touch, but the ability has never activated itself like this before."

"I feel different," Nero said. "As if I could run the entire length of the forest and lift this house on my own."

"Me, too… Well, not lifting a house or running. Never been a jogger, but I'd go three more rounds of sex." I laughed and my cheeks burned up. *Had I said that out loud?*

Nero chuckled and pushed the hair off my cheek. "I don't

know what you've done to me, but, if this is your ability, fuck, I want more."

With a final kiss on my brow, he broke free and picked up my clothes, handing them to me. "The bathroom is across the hallway. Let me make you a cup of tea."

With the clothes bunched up in my arms, I nodded, even though Nero had already turned toward the fireplace. So I spun and hurried over the cold floorboards. A quick look showed no sign of the wolf. I sprinted into the bathroom. The room had a real toilet with plumbing. Holy moly... they liked their creature comforts. In haste, I cleaned myself, got dressed, and stopped at the door, gripping the handle.

"Okay, what now?" I mumbled to myself, still floating on the heated excitement from having the most stupendous sex with a wolf shifter. And I wasn't ready to walk away from him. Sure, I was still stuck in the house until I cured Dagen, and the dark wolf looked ready to bite my head off, but Nero was doing something to me and I ached for more.

Going home was a must so I could clear my mind, yet a tightness strangled my chest at the thought of walking away from Nero. But what was I supposed to do? How would something between us work? We'd cross the border to go out on dates? He was an alpha, and who knew where his jurisdiction lay. Miles away perhaps, as he'd said Oryn controlled the territory next to Terra.

This was insane. I clearly got caught up in the moment, let myself go wild, but now I had think straight. I was in enemy territory, and I wouldn't be safe until I left. Plus, there was no future with me and any shifter. Goddess, their kind killed my parents.

The solution was to grill Nero, find out everything about the Den, then make a decision on how I'd leave. Even convince him that I had to go home for herbs to heal Dagen. Maybe he ought to join me. But going back wasn't safe for me with the priestess on the prowl, let along taking a wolf shifter into Terra. Heaviness settled in my stomach at how complicated everything was getting.

Since arriving, he'd fed me and brought me to two orgasms. Heavens, I wasn't his prisoner. What were we doing?

Squaring my shoulders, I opened the door and marched into the kitchen, ready to follow through with my plan. But what I found was the door across the room wide open and sunshine pouring in. The woods spread outward, greenery in bloom, sun glistening off the leaves.

Freedom.

Nero wasn't anywhere in sight. Was he outdoors? I sprinted through the kitchen and burst outside, but the moment I rounded the corner of the wooden house, I came face to face with the black wolf—Oryn. The hair on his nape rose and he unleashed a gravelly snarl.

A yelp fell from my throat, and I retreated, hitting the wall with my back, terror biting into my flesh, insisting this was where I'd die.

CHAPTER 7

The edges of my mind frayed, and I kept telling myself Oryn was a shifter. Inside him lay his humanity, yet staring at the wolf growling at me, trepidation shook me at the core. He lowered his head, and the breeze fluffed the black fur across his shoulder bones.

"L-Listen, I'm not a danger to you," I said. "You're the one with long teeth. And pointy ears, so you'd hear me if I tried to sneak up on you to hurt you. Please."

He shifted closer, blocking off the easy path for me to dart back into the house.

I slid along the outside wooden wall of the house in the opposite direction, but he snapped at the air between us, and I coiled in on myself. "I just want to go home."

But he wasn't backing away, and showing weakness drove wolves to attack, right? I wasn't a helpless bunny in shock. I straightened myself and swallowed the rock in my throat.

Wolves were all about dominance and Nero had said the three of them were alphas, so I wouldn't back down. Or was it I should never stare them in the eyes? I couldn't remember when I had zero control over even trembling.

Oryn's ears perked and swiveled toward the side of the house as if he'd heard something.

"I didn't mean to enter your territory, but I was running for my life. And then I fell off this cliff." I was rambling, and my pulse sped as a deep guttural snarl boomed from his chest.

"If I'd had any other option, trust me, this would be the last place I'd visit." I hugged myself, scanning the woodland around us. No sign of a track, just endless pines. Though the gurgle of the river reached me. I had to find a way back up the sharp cliff I'd fallen over and back home.

He watched me with intelligence behind his gaze. Was he remembering Nero and me doing the vertical dance in his kitchen? I burned from the inside out at turning into a nympho, but I didn't need anyone else judging me. I did a good enough job myself.

"What you saw in the kitchen... Well..." My mouth parched. Heavens, how would I ever explain the birds and bees to my kids when I burned up with embarrassment talking about the topic? Let alone, I didn't understand how attracted I was so easily to Nero, how he affected me, or how I could have allowed him to take me like that. Maybe this whole land was making me crazy.

Oryn's head jerked over his shoulder, and he charged in that direction, kicking dirt in his wake. He vanished around the corner of the cabin.

For those few moments, I froze on the spot, gulping for air. Leave or stay? Part of me insisted I return to the house and remain safe from wild wolves. Except, Nero said they'd dealt with the wolf that attacked me. And who said I was protected from the three alphas in the cabin? Oryn looked ready to tear me apart. And what if Nero coming onto me was a guise to trick me into becoming their sex slaves?

I had to trust my gut instincts which screamed I run

home. So, I spun in the opposite direction and sprinted away from the house.

The ground flew beneath my steps as I ran in and out around trees, leaping over shrubs and dead branches. Evergreens tugged on my trousers, but I didn't care. Not when the sloshing of water grew louder. What if I found a way down the cascade…? There might be an easier way to cross the river and get back up the terrain toward home. Santos would worry about me, and that was if the priestess hadn't locked him up because of me. Those thoughts had me running faster.

Ahead, light pierced the thick canopy, and I charged, bursting from the stranglehold of trees to a ledge that over-looked the stream at least thirty feet below. Catching my breath, I gawked at the roaring waterfall, a fine mist suspended over the water.

Sharp stones flanked the cliffs with no easy way to scale down, and considering I'd barely survived the first fall, I wasn't tempting fate again.

Multiple howls ricocheted through the woods, and I flinched. Were Oryn and Nero now hunting me? As much as part of me craved more of Nero, was I being foolish in believing anything was possible? He was a shifter and his kind had killed my parents. Grandma had confirmed she'd witnessed the whole attack. So what would stop them from butchering me after I healed Dagen? Was that Oryn's inten-tion? Or Nero would use me as his sex slave? The latter should have terrified me, but it flooded my gut with tingles. Geez, what was wrong with me?

I raced alongside the cliff's edge. The land sloped, meaning it might bring me down to the rapids. From there, I'd swim across and dilute my scent so I'd lose my pursuers.

My feet slid out from under me. I screamed and fell to my

side, groaning as my hip hit a boulder. I winced from the sharp pain shooting up my back.

A repetitive tapping of paws against soil grew closer, louder. I scrambled to my feet.

The forest blurred past as I sprinted downhill.

Another howl had me glancing over my shoulder. Behind me, four wolves charged after me.

Wait. Four?

My head spun and every inch of me froze. My breath wouldn't come.

It wasn't Oryn. These hounds were brown.

I dashed down the hill, a cry flying from my throat. Were these real wolves or shifters? Why were they chasing me? Of course, I knew… to eat me.

Swinging away, I spotted the fiends closing in from either side of me.

Leaving the house had been dumb. How I hated hindsight, because I seemed to be the queen of making mistakes.

Footfalls closed in.

My heart galloped, and I scanned the area for any trees to scale.

One wolf lunged from my left, and I ducked. Something blurred and crashed into the attacking animal, both rolling around.

It was Oryn; his black fur and larger size confirmed it. What was he doing saving me? So he could force me back to the house as his prisoner and personal medical caretaker?

I darted forward, but the next wolf was on me. I grabbed a branch off the ground and spun fast, swinging the weapon, catching the hound across the head.

Another came at me, fur bristled, fangs bared and salivating. Wildness inhabited its gaze.

I jabbed my stick into his ribs, driving the mutt away, and swung at the third one. All three of them fanned out in front of me, a tree at my back, foliage my only ammunition.

Holy heavens. My lungs refused to function.

"If any of you are shifters, let's talk about this." I crouched in slow motion, collecting a big rock. A quick glance behind me revealed woods as far as I could see.

The bigger wolf in the middle stepped closer, its head low.

A numbing sensation engulfed me, paralyzing me to the spot. Was this how my parents had felt when they'd faced off a pack and died? What chance did I have?

My pulse was a drum in my skull. Grandma had always told me to fight for what I believed in and, damn, I wasn't ready to leave this world.

When the other two wolves approached, I hurled the stone at the larger one, nicking an ear, and it snapped. I jabbed the other wolf's snout, but he seized the stick and bit through it.

A dark form shot forward from my left, and the giant brown wolf swung to face off with Oryn. Both wolves knitted in a brawl, fur flying off.

I whirled, jumped up to a low-hanging branch, and threw my legs up.

Something snagged my pants, ripping the fabric from my butt and tugging the material down my leg. A wolf's teeth. The creature dragged me back down.

The scream caught in my chest burst free. My fingers slipped, and I imagined myself falling into the mutt's jaws, ripped to shreds.

I kicked the hound in the nose on the way down, loosening him. The second wolf latched on to my other leg, teeth piercing flesh. Screaming didn't help.

I tensed, my arms flailing.

Two wolves faced me.

When a third opponent staggered toward us, I gasped as I recognized Oryn. Blood matted his mangled fur and dripped from one ear. His snarl had both wolves snapping toward him and, without hesitation, they both attacked him.

I turned to run but stopped at the sounds of whimpers and growls.

Oryn had protected me, and I'd never walked away from injured animals or those in need.

I picked up another piece of wood and rushed toward the brawl. Not thinking, I brought the weapon down on one hound's rump. It released its hold of Oryn's front leg. "Leave him alone." I jammed the end of the stick right into his mouth. He stumbled sideways, choking, as I yanked the stick back.

"Get out of here," I called out to scare it away.

When it didn't, I jabbed it once more in the neck, stepping closer, and at once the beast retreated.

Yes, I'd stood up to a wolf!

I whirled around.

But a huge form struck me in the stomach. The air gushed from my lungs, and I tumbled backward.

Another wolf's incisors hovered inches from my face, drooling on my chin. I shuddered, dread swallowing me.

I didn't remember bucking, but I fought with every ounce of strength, shoving against the assault. The animal flew off me in a flash, and there stood Oryn as a wolf, bleeding, one leg bent. I pushed myself up and approached him. With a shaky hand, I touched a wound on his back. A zip of energy skipped from my finger and across his back. What was up with my ability?

He jolted as if I'd shocked him. With a growl, he lifted his chin, pointing back toward the house.

Leave now. I got it.

Wrenching myself backward, I ran, my thighs aching. Nothing would stop me.

On my next step, the ground beneath me gave way. I fell forward into a hole that opened before me. Darkness swallowed me, and I screamed until I hit hard soil at the base of the pit.

I swore every bone in my body had broken. Why in the world was there a hole in the mountain? Who were wolves trying to catch? A boar? The hounds seemed more the hunting type.

Escalating grunts came from somewhere above. I massaged the ache across my temple. The opening lay at least twice my height above me. And for the first time since getting lost, tears prickled my eyes. Everything I did turned to crap. Each turn brought me closer to death. There was a reason Grandma had warned me about the Den, and now I wasn't sure if I had chosen the lesser evil by running from the priestess.

I staggered to my feet and searched for anything to help me escape. Tree roots stuck out of the walls, and I pulled hard on one. The root didn't snap. *Perfect.* Damn this, I was getting out of this territory alive and nothing would get in my way. Digging my boot into the wall for a footing, I clambered upward. I had scaled rock faces before with Bee when we'd gone exploring in the woods.

My grip slipped.

I lost my balance. Panicked, I reached for anything.

A shadow hovered over me, and a hand seized my wrist. I flew out of the pit with such speed my stomach lurched.

Falling to my knees, I was a couple of feet away from a naked man. His skin was sun-kissed, and he cradled an arm across his chest. Bite marks littered his body. A gash beneath his eye bled down his cheek. Blood marred an injured ear.

"Oryn?" Even with injuries and him wavering on his feet,

the man was bigger than Nero. Long, dark hair framed the bluest eyes and his strong jawline, and my gaze fell to his lips and the broadness of his shoulders. Yep, all the single girls had to do was visit the Den if they wanted to search for a hunk to call their own. But that meant meandering through the dangers of savage wolves.

He stared at me with a desperation in his gaze and nodded once before his knees buckled. He crashed to the ground, landing on his side.

I rushed to his side. "Oryn, how bad are you hurt?"

He moaned and wasn't rushing to get up. Around me lay two other wolves, bloodied and unmoving. Oryn had risked his life for me, fighting four wolves. Sure, if I yearned to run away, this was the time. Yet I couldn't bring myself to leave him vulnerable. Any predators that found him would make a meal of him. The priestess forcing everyone to stay away from the wolves' territory was a blessing in disguise.

A distant howl echoed.

I shuddered. *Oh, crap!*

CHAPTER 8

*a*nother howl came, piercing and threatening. I'd heard wolf songs often when in the forest and how tranquil they'd always sounded.

Oryn pushed himself up from the ground, a grunt rolling through his chest. He looked down at himself as if he'd never seen himself as a human before. Surely not. Nero had said all three were alpha shifters.

"Why are wolves attacking you?" I glanced over my shoulder at the thick woods, shadows crowding between the trunks. I was convinced I'd see an army of hounds rushing down the hill to rip us apart.

"Sharlot," Oryn responded, his voice deep and guttural, carrying accent I couldn't detect lining his words.

I grabbed his arm, forcing him to move. Standing around would get us killed.

"My name is Scarlet." Heavens... or did he mean "harlot"? After all, he'd watched Nero and me going at it. My face heated, and I looked away, ready to crawl under a rock.

He seized my forearm and drew me toward him with such force, I tripped and fell against him, my palms snapping

75

against a hard, bare chest, scorching hot beneath my touch. I gasped and peered up into the bluest eyes, framed by long, dark lashes, crowned by heavy brows.

"What have you done?" His fingers dug into my arm.

Fire burned through me. I hadn't just survived wolf attacks to have my savior turn on me. Or had that been his intention all along? "What are you talking about?"

I wrenched against his hold, but I might as well have been in a tug-o-war with a boulder.

"What magic did you use to return me to a human?"

"I didn't do anything. Maybe you changed yourself?"

He shook his head. "Nope. I was stuck in my wolf form."

Another howl, and Oryn lifted his chin, sniffing the air.

I scanned the surrounding trees. "We need to go before more of them come."

Oryn pushed into a march while holding on to my arm, and I limped alongside him, rubbing the bruises forming along my hip from the earlier fall.

"Hey, let go," I said. "You'll cover more ground on your own."

"No! You helped me and I *will* keep you protected."

All right, not that I could say *no* to getting bodyguard action from a hunk, but why were we headed away from the house? "Aren't we going the wrong way? The house is up the hill."

I staggered alongside him as his pace picked up.

"There's more coming from that direction. We need to hide our scent and wait for them to leave." He rushed, and he took me with him.

I wasn't sure how to take Oryn, not with his stiff demeanor and the commanding way he spoke without a hint of emotion. Was that how he ran his pack, all demands and controls? Damn, his members must be warriors. Then again, Nero had said this part of the Den belonged to Oryn, so did that mean he had just fought his own pack? Why would they attack him? And why had he been stuck as a wolf?

Grunts came from farther behind us, and Oryn increased his pace. His once-injured arm now swung easily by his side. How quickly did these shifters heal?

Apparently fast, so why hadn't Dagen woken up yet?

Didn't matter. All those questions had to wait until we weren't in danger. When Oryn broke into a run, he dragged me with him.

The gushing sound of running water reached me, and the more ground we covered, the louder the sound grew. We emerged near the river bank. The roaring crash of the water-fall stood to our left. Above was where I'd fallen off the cliff. Good to know I'd headed in the right direction in my attempt to escape. Which had failed miserably.

A plume of water vapor hung over the pool and, if I wasn't running for my life, I might consider sitting here for hours with my paints and canvas, capturing this beauty.

"Get undressed," Oryn broke through my thoughts, letting go of my arm and pulling at my sleeve.

"Hey." I slapped his hand away. "Don't manhandle me. Understand? And no one is taking my clothes off but me." And Nero, it seemed. *Crap*.

"Sharlot, this—"

"It's Scarlet." I rolled my eyes.

"Your garments carry your scent and will slow us down. We need a distraction."

My pulse was racing as I looked back, praying the wolves weren't close. Oryn stood there, his gaze wild. Yet mine dipped down his body because I had zero control. *Oh, sweet heavens*. He was bigger than Nero in the downstairs department!

"Hurry. Later you will have plenty of time to study me."

I arched a brow and looked up as the corner of his mouth

turned upward. For the love of wolfsbane, he had me burning up, and I turned away, unbuttoning my vest. Yep, because my options were either face the wolves or get into the river. Though I had no idea why I had to get naked. When I twisted to protest, Oryn towered over me.

"Quickly, Sharlot."

I sighed, clear he wasn't going to pronounce my name correctly, and I somehow suspected with his light accent, he was trying this best.

The snap of foliage came from within the woodland, and I toed off my boots, then pulled off my shirt, pants, and underwear.

Oryn reached over and grabbed my belongings before bunching them into a ball and running down the bank at least fifteen feet. He then tossed them into the forest and my boots farther away.

"Those were my favorite boots," I mumbled to myself.

A grunt sounded louder from somewhere near.

I twitched and spun, searching for the culprit.

Oryn snatched my wrist and hauled me into the river. "Quick."

I covered my breasts with an arm, and a scream of protest wedged in my throat for agreeing to lose my clothes and remain naked in the wolves' territory. But getting eaten wasn't an option, and when the heavy snarls emerged from within the forest, I moved with haste.

Oryn smiled but didn't say a word as he drew me deeper. Iciness lapped to my waist, and the pebbly river bottom stabbed my feet. I winced. He leaned over, slid a hand under my knees and another behind my back, lifting me off my feet, and cradled me in his arms.

The air gushed from my lungs. We pressed against each other, naked. He kept moving, the coldness splashing up and over my stomach.

I shivered. "I c-can w-walk."

"You're too slow. Now hold on."

I pulled my gaze from Oryn and noticed we were headed toward the edge of the waterfall, where the cascade thinned. Too terrified to argue, I hugged his neck, staring at the river behind us.

"I'll keep you safe. Trust me," Oryn whispered in my ear, and his soft words uncoiled the knot in my gut. I held on to him tight and stared at the bank where the first shape of a wolf had appeared. Would he see us?

As we pushed beneath the waterfall, a sudden explosion of ice cold water pummeled my side, my back, my head. I tucked myself against Oryn's neck, nestled in his arms. The sensation was like a mountain pressing down on me.

I flinched as the crashing water suffocated me, compressing me.

But his arms squeezed me to him and, soon enough, the agonizing beating eased.

"Are you all right?" he asked.

I lifted my head, shaking with cold, and met his concerned expression. We now stood behind the waterfall in a cave. "That was terrifying."

"We're safe here. The wolves won't risk the flow of the waterfall."

When he lowered my feet into a small lagoon that reached my thighs, he climbed out onto the rocky edge. His tight ass caught my attention, along with his strong legs and his muscles moving beneath his skin. Who was this hunter? He strode forward into the mouth of darkness, leaving me alone.

"Hello, Oryn?" My words shook, and I hated that I showed fear. I followed and a frostiness settled in my bones. Yep and my nudity wasn't helping one bit... though body heat would help. I sounded more like Bee every day.

A glint flicked from deeper inside the cave and, at once, a golden flame illuminated at the rear. Shadows leaped across his face as he crouched near the fire set up on a premade bed of branches surrounded by a circle of rocks.

"Is this your place?" I called out over the roaring waterfall behind me as I approached him, loving the warmth already radiating from the blaze. Yet a chill still spiraled up my spine from the opening at my back, and freezing droplets rolled over my shoulders from my hair.

"It's one of my rest places." He walked to a wall and returned with a blanket and something else in his other hand. "Dry yourself."

I didn't protest and pulled the thick fabric over my shoulders and crouched near the fire. "Thank you. Why do you have a blanket here?"

Oryn also handed me a dried strip of meat, which I accepted. "I don't usually spend every second of the day in my wolf form, and it gets cold in winter."

Yesterday had been a regular day at my store. Now, I was in Den territory, and I'd met three wolf shifters, made one unconscious, had sex with another, and was now stuck in a cave, naked, with the third. I had zero idea how to even get out of this situation, and huge problems awaited me once I returned home.

"So, what is your business in our territory?" Oryn asked, sitting with his knees bent to his chest, as he bit into a meat strip.

"It wasn't my intention. I ran toward here to escape capture, then I fell off a cliff and ended up in the river. The rest is history, I guess."

"Who was after you and why? Are you a criminal?" He studied me as if I were a microscopic insect just recently discovered.

"Ha, you're funny. I have never stolen anything in my life

or hurt anyone, either. But I witnessed something I shouldn't have, and now the priestess wants to imprison me, probably for life. She's part royalty—did you know?—so no one can overthrow her decision while she rules over Terra. My protests would get ignored, and I need a plan."

He broke off a chunk and nodded as he chewed. Blood wove down his arm and he wiped the cut beneath his eye.

"Let me tend to your wounds?" I offered.

"I'll be fine. These are nothing."

I moved closer to him. "I insist." Though I didn't have my bag or any herbs. "Do you have any material I can use? The cut on your arm is deep and at least let's try to stop that."

He shrugged and his chin pointed to the wall across from the fire. I climbed up and found shelves dug into the rock surface with another bunched up blanket and what looked like a shirt, but when I pulled it out, it was half a bed sheet. Okay, this would do, so I tore off one end with my teeth and shredded it into long strips.

I kneeled next to Oryn and wiped the blood with the material. "Thanks for saving me earlier. You took on four wolves. That's insane."

He chuckled as if his mind were miles away, and, considering the dozens of healed scars on his body, just like on Dagen's, it might have been an ordinary fight for him.

"I survived." He took another bite of his meal.

"Why did you save me?"

He chewed on his food. "Can't explain it, you just smelled different to me. Sweet and alluring. And my wolf insisted."

"So I guess it's normal for an alpha to face death every day? Sounds horrifying. Not sure I'd want to be looking over my shoulder every moment of the day, not knowing if today would be my last." Why would anyone be an alpha?

He shrugged. "Is there any other way?"

I sat on my heels. "Of course. Don't you have time away

from being in charge when you can sleep in, go for a stroll in the afternoon, just laugh and not always be on guard?"

He twisted to look at me with an arched brow, his nose red from the cold. "Strolling? Is that what you do in Terra?"

"Sometimes. My grandma used to say life wasn't worth living if you didn't make time for family and friends."

Oryn scoffed and scrunched his nose.

"Don't be rude if you don't agree." I wiped more blood dripping down his arm and wrapped his wound, pulling the fabric tight. Then I cleaned the bite mark across his ear, though it had already stopped bleeding.

He cleared his throat loudly. "I grew up being told if I wanted to survive, I had to fight for everything. Never show weakness."

"That's harsh. Your parents—"

"No." He cut me off with a stern look. "They deserved the death they got. They abandoned me at four years old, then my adoptive parents did the same when I was eight. But I made my way to the alpha position. The Den is harsh; everyone here accepts that. So don't pity me."

I swallowed the rest of my words and tied up the loose end of his bandage. We sat in silence, him brooding and staring into the fire. I changed the topic.

"Why did those wolves attack us? Aren't they part of your pack? Nero told me this was your territory."

Oryn licked his lips, arms resting on bent knees, his shoulders slouched forward, yet my gaze traced the number of new cuts over the healed scars. He might have had a hard upbringing, facing abandonment, but something inside me *did* pity him. It was nothing I'd admit out loud, but for him to believe his only path in life was to never back down was a horrendous way to live. For his sanity, for his future, and for all the things he would miss out on, I hoped he opened his eyes to doing more with his life. But then again, what did I know about how packs lived in the Den? Yet Nero didn't have this world-against-him approach and he was an alpha too.

"Those wolves that attacked us are from my pack," Oryn began. "Over a week ago, everyone started acting strange. Aggressive, stuck in their wolf forms, and attacking each other. I was the same, locked as my wolf, but not as lost to my wild side as the others." He glanced over at me, his lips pinched. "Until you touched me. It was like a lightning strike, and I felt the shift inside me, unlocking my human side."

He studied me, tracing the length of my body as I tucked the blanket across my chest in the style of a dress. "How did you do that?"

"Don't know what I did. I was panicked and just touched you. It's never happened before." The sensation had struck me, too, just as it had with Nero, and I hadn't given it a thought when my focus had been on surviving.

He took my hand in his, studying my fingertips. "You're different. Not like other humans I've seen. Cutting down trees, planting wolfsbane into our land."

I stiffened. "You've seen them, too? That's what I saw the priestess doing this morning and her guards chased me into the Den." I huffed. "I didn't know why she was transporting and replanting wolfsbane into your land."

Oryn's upper lip curled, reminding me of when he was in wolf form. "I know what she was doing. Stealing our land by extending the line of wolfsbane. Seen it myself."

I hugged myself. The priestess had always hated wolves, declaring them demons at every town gathering and threatening to eradicate them. But she'd been saying it for so long that everyone put it down to her obsession. No one had expected her to *act* on it. Except I'd witnessed her ordering wolfsbane into wolf territory.

"What she's doing is wrong. Can't you stop her?" I asked,

well aware that over a century ago, the leaders of each race in Haven had come together and agreed to split Haven for the sake of ending the bloodshed. And for years, everyone had remained in their own realms in harmony. So why was the priestess disturbing the balance?

"That was the plan when I first discovered her actions. But then my pack acted weird, and my priority turned to helping them." Shadows crowded under his eyes, darkening his expression.

"That's why Nero and Dagen are in your house, isn't it? To help with your pack. Are they your brothers?"

"Yes, they are helping me. The three of us have been friends since before we became alphas. We met at the annual hunter meet. I stumbled on Dagen cornered by a huge bear that had come down from the mountains. So I jumped in to help him and, halfway through, Nero burst into our fight. We scared the bear off our lands and bonded, friends ever since."

That reminded me of the time I had wandered in the woods behind my place after my grandma had passed. I hadn't been sure life was worth living, and I'd felt lost, alone. I'd slept for a week straight out in the forest. Bee had found me as she'd searched for ingredients to heal her father from a burn. We'd chatted about her potion, and I'd suggested using the aloe vera, as it carried strong healing properties for burns. I hadn't cared that she'd seen me use my ability on the plant, and that was when she'd told me she practiced magic. So I'd joined her, and together we'd healed her dad. Then we'd become inseparable.

"Sometimes," I said, "when a stranger helps you for no reason, that action can ignite the most incredible friendship."

He nodded. "So, what did you do to Dagen?"

Okay, his question had come out of the blue, but it wasn't surprising. I gave him an explanation of how my citrus spray had gotten tangled with the wolfsbane and it might have been what had knocked out Dagen.

"Wait!" His voice darkened, and he twisted to face me. "You brought wolfsbane into my home?"

An icy chill captured me. "Didn't you hear me? I didn't enter the Den on purpose."

"How do I know you're not working for the priestess? Over the months, I've seen you several times near the border of our lands, picking wolfsbane."

"That was you? I knew I felt someone watching me. But I'm not working for the priestess. I'm an apothecary. If I wanted to hurt you, I would have used the wolfsbane in the house on all three of you and killed you already." Hmm, okay, I hadn't meant to sound threatening, but Oryn had driven my response.

His snarl hung in the air, and he trembled. "I was wrong to trust you."

"It wasn't as if I had time to think when I was running for my life." I leaned away from him. "You attacked me, remember?" My muscles flexed.

His fingers twitched against the stone ground between us. Would he transform into his wolf? What if he lost control like his pack and killed me?

I gulped for air. "Look, I would never harm you or any of the wolves. I just want to return home and I pray the priestess hasn't burned down my herbal store."

Oryn's body shuddered, and his pupils vanished upward, leaving only the whites of his eyes.

I scrambled to my feet and retreated. "Oh, crap, you're turning, aren't you? Please don't. Please."

Retreating to the entrance, where sprinkles of water struck me from above, I peered out from a tiny gap near the curtain of water. Two wolves fought over my pants. That could end up being me.

I turned to find Oryn on hands and knees, his spine arching.

My heart pounded against my ribcage. If I was to ever experience a stroke, this was the time.

But I'd helped him transform with a touch before. At first, my legs refused to budge, but I couldn't do nothing. I bit down on my lower lip and hurried closer. With a shaking hand, I reached over and touched his arm. He snapped around, growling, his teeth elongating.

I jumped backward. "Fuck!" I cursed.

Oryn raised himself on two feet, convulsing. A strangled, broken howl burst from his throat.

Shit, the other wolves would hear, and... I rushed toward him, despite shaking like a leaf, and slapped a hand over his mouth. "Be quiet!"

He pushed my hand away and stepped toward me, holding on to my shoulders, his eyes wild. His teeth were normal-sized, but his skin shimmered.

I retreated, and a strangled cry pressed on my chest. I hit the wall. A tiny cry flew past my throat. "Oryn, please."

He smirked, as if my fear turned him on. *Bastard.*

"Sharlot," he growled, and as much as it annoyed me how he pronounced my name, at the moment I worried more about him ripping out my throat.

He quivered against me. His emotions filtered across his face, from terror to a starved hunger.

"Don't do this. I'm not food or your enemy." A spark coiled across my fingers.

A deep guttural rumble sounded through him, and his grip on my arm tightened.

I ground my teeth, shallow pants feeding my lungs.

His exhales brushed against me, his chest rising and falling faster.

He lurched closer, and I turned away as he sniffed my neck.

I held on to a scream.

"Mine," he demanded.

That single word unraveled the tightness in my gut, and a river of warmth cascaded through me just as it had with Nero. An insatiable desire claimed me, throttled me.

Oryn remained inches from me, unblinking. His dark side left me shaken. I lifted my free hand and placed the palm against his chest, the static from my fingers sizzling and bouncing across his flesh.

He shuddered backward from my touch and unleashed a snarl.

I snatched Oryn's arm and kept him upright. "Hey, I've got you."

His eyes shifted to the brightest blues... gone was his wolf, and only the man remained. "What are you?"

CHAPTER 9

"I'm a normal person," I answered, but Oryn lifted my knuckles to his nose, sniffing them.

"Fire. Burnt wood. Makes the hair on my arms stand on end." Yet his fingers intertwined with mine. "How did you make my wolf retreat again?"

My attempt to focus left me fogged as my focal point remained on our joined palms and the desire to snuggle closer, crawl into his embrace, and have him tell me again how I was his.

Heavens, what was wrong with me? How could both Nero and Oryn drive me wild? Or did all wolves have this effect on humans? Oryn rubbed the back of my hand with a thumb, reminding me he waited for an answer.

"I've always been able to amplify the strength of herbs, but I don't understand why my touch affects you. If it helps, that's a good thing, right?"

He nodded and a lock of his black hair draped over his face. I reached over and pushed it aside, but he caught my wrist and inhaled my scent. "The sweetest flower floats behind the electric scent. It calls to my wolf, but it shouldn't." Oryn dropped my arm and drew away.

"Why not?" The same magnetic pull I'd had with Nero now drew me to Oryn as if a cord kept us together, and the distance between us ached deep in my chest. My attraction made no sense, but I kept trailing after him.

He jerked around, stopping me in my tracks near the entrance, the lagoon in the cave rippling from the waterfall about fifteen feet away. "Because we're from different worlds. As a human, even with magic, you're not supposed to affect my wolf."

An icy breeze from outside brushed against me and goosebumps coated my skin. "But you felt something, right? Just like me." I raised my voice over the cascade. And like with Nero.

"I can't offer you anything," he replied.

Stiffening, I crossed my arms. "I'm not asking you for anything. Just trying to understand what's happening to us." I turned away, fire hitting my cheeks. Who did he think he was? Heavens, I came across as a desperate girl instead of reining in my emotions, my urges. Everything in the Den twisted me inside out and shoved aside logic. I loved order and rational thinking, but I seemed to have left those back home. And just thinking of my store and Santos had worry slithering through my stomach. Was he okay? And I'd let Bee down by not supplying her wolfsbane in time. And how would I ever make it home alive?

Sunlight glinted through the watery curtain, and, for a few moments, I mistook the view for tranquility. The explosion of grunts and barks from outside killed that fantasy.

"We're not going anywhere for a while," Oryn said as he retreated into the cave, taking a seat next to the fire.

With a long exhale, I stood there, frustration worming through me. "I need to get home."

"Good luck."

His response had me tensing, and I spun to face him. "What is your problem? Is it me—because I'm a human?"

"I don't know you," he snapped, "but you helped me break out of my wolf form, and for that I'll get you back to my house."

Chewing on a hangnail, I studied the way he never blinked while holding my stare. Was that how he dealt with everyone... intimidating them into submission? "Can you take me to the human border instead?"

"No. We won't make it that far with my pack in attack mode." He ran a hand through his long hair and turned away, facing the fire. "The wolves out there are my family and I don't want to hurt them if possible, so I'll do what it takes to avoid that." When he spun around, his expression hardened. "Your touch. Would it work on my wolves?"

"No idea. I didn't even know it would help you. My ability amplifies herbs and has never impacted a person before." Except he wasn't a normal person, but a wolf shifter. "Who knows? It might."

"Once it quiets outside, I'll capture a wolf and bring him to you to try. Deal?"

A sudden coldness tightened around my lungs. "Wouldn't you be giving away our location? What if it bit me?"

"We'll do it outdoors once most of the wolves leave. Until then, rest."

I joined him and warmed up by the flames. The silence turned awkward despite the fact that earlier I'd been contemplating jumping into his arms like a crazed, horny beast. This wasn't me in the slightest. I didn't kiss boys on the first date, let alone allow them to get me to hang from the ceiling while they brought me to orgasm. My cheeks burned at the memory. This might be normal for wolves—fight and have sex day in and out. Though the latter wouldn't be too bad if all the shifters resembled the three I'd encountered.

With a deep inhale, I glanced around at the space at the rear of the cave. "Is this place your getaway? Your special place?"

He twisted toward me, a brow arched, and only then did I realize the double meaning behind my words. "This is my private sanctuary. You're the first I've brought here."

"Ah, nice." I took in my surroundings. "Explains why you've got no decorating."

"Only humans need objects to feel fulfilled."

"Hey," I said. "That's not true. Sometimes objects carry sentimental attachments. Like the red cloak my grandma left me, but it got torn. Every time I used it, I swear I sensed her presence."

Silence filled the void once more, and I crossed my legs, studying my fingers and the dirt wedged under my nails.

"You were close with your grandma?" he asked.

"Absolutely. She raised me after wolves killed my parents." I paused, regretting my words, but when he didn't make a comment, I continued. "She taught me everything from cooking apple pie to memorizing different herbs." I brushed away a dead leaf stuck to my big toe. "A day doesn't pass when I don't miss her. I keep worrying that one day I'll forget what her voice sounded like, what she looked like."

"Some say those you love will remain in your heart, so she will always be with you." He stared into the fire as he spoke and the first trickle of emotion flickered beneath his tone.

"Thank you. That's real sweet. You seem close to your pack... do you consider them a family? Is that how it works in the Den?" I recalled him saying his parents were dead, but everyone needed someone to look out for them.

"I'd do anything to protect them."

Oryn didn't strike me as a person who got all emotional,

but it was clear he loved his clan, so regardless of what his mom and dad had done to him, he'd found a new bond. And his determination to keep them safe showed him to be a caring man... the opposite of what I'd suspected when I'd first met him.

"I have that kind of connection with a few friends."

When silence fell over us again, I racked my brain for a topic of conversation, something to fill the emptiness that reminded me of my troubles, how alone I was in the Den, and how I now wore no clothes. I drew the blanket tighter under my arms.

"Why does your house have no windows?"

He huffed into a chuckle, and the sound calmed me. While the broody expression gave him an air of mystery, seeing him laugh made him super sexy, and left me covered in goosebumps.

"Dagen bugs me about that all the time. He loves natural light, but the place is a resting home, a location to lie low if I need a hiding spot. Plus, windows are much easier to break in to than bolted doors."

"Break in? Who would do that? Wolves in other packs?"

"No. Bears and even lion shifters enter our land. Scouts come here to scope out potential takeovers. And sometimes a wolf gets cornered, so I built cabins all over the territory with weapons or medical supplies in case they were needed."

I shifted to face him. "Wow. That is so nice of you."

"Does it surprise you to discover we're not savages?" His voice carried a playful tone, as if proud of proving me wrong.

Leaning back on both arms, I stretched my legs out in front of me, the blaze casting an orange hue across my shins and the blanket reaching halfway up my thighs. "What do hunters think of humans?"

He inched toward me, shadows dancing under the darkened bruise beneath his eye. "That you're skittish of anything that moves and are warmongers."

"That's harsh. I'm not scared of the forest. Well, okay, wolves and bears—"

"And you're most likely to make yourselves extinct by infighting than any other race."

"Is everyone taking bets on that?" Hmm, I had to agree with that, considering how the priestess treated her own kind. Oryn built sheltered homes for his pack, while she imprisoned us if we didn't follow her strict rules.

"Yep."

Geez, *we* were the savages. "How many members are in your pack?" I asked.

"On last count, three hundred and thirty-seven. Though we've had a few births, so that number's gone up."

"Wow. Are they safe at the moment?"

He nodded. "The young pups aren't affected, and I sent them to Dagen's pack until we sorted out our mess. It seems only my pack is impacted."

"Have you narrowed down the cause?" I asked, remembering a story about a pride of lion shifters falling sick all at once. Turned out a huge kill that had fed the entire clan had eaten a poisonous plant. The pride had passed away. "Did you have a huge party recently, everyone eating the same kill? Or plants?"

Wolfsbane? That wouldn't turn the wolves feral but would have made them ill, knocked them out as my own wolfsbane had done to Dagen. That memory had my gut twisting in on itself.

He shook his head. "Nothing like that. But I'll find out what's going on and make things right again," he said.

"I love how much you care for them. It reminds me of my grandma in so many ways—putting others first."

"There's no other way when so many lives are under my protection."

His response struck a chord because I'd been raised to aid a person in need; that was why I'd never turned someone away from the store. Initially, Oryn might have terrified me, but now I couldn't help but notice the similarities between us. We'd both lost our families and would do anything for those we had left. And his habit of pushing others away made sense. He was always in guard mode... and that made me admire him but also wonder when he'd burn out.

We sat there, chatting about everything from my favorite herbs to the best game he'd hunted. Any other time and place, and we'd have made fantastic friends. He laughed, the sound warming me. Who was I kidding...? Definitely more than friends.

He marched to the cave's opening and nightfall already cloaked the land.

"They're still out there."

My hopes dwindled. "Tossing my clothes so close to our location wasn't a great idea then."

"Wolves hunt at night, and your garments will make them focus on something other than attacking each other. We'll leave at first light. Let's get some sleep." He moved to the back of the cave and returned with something long and cylindrical under his arm. He unraveled one end, letting it fall to his feet to reveal a rug and several blankets tucked inside. In haste, he laid them on the floor in the rear.

I wasn't sure I could sleep while my thoughts rushed. "What if a wolf finds our spot while we sleep?"

"No wolf would ever enter the river or go near the waterfall while in animal form, as they're afraid of drowning under the cascade. A few miles down the river, the waters are shallow and almost still. That's where they drink and wash.

Not here." Oryn tapped the bed he'd created and waved me over.

Heavens, all my worries slipped into the abyss and were replaced with the image of a naked hunk calling me to bed with him. The earlier tingles twirled in my stomach, and I approached him, then crawled across the rug and blankets, a bit clammy to the touch. But it was better than the stone ground.

He lay on his back and stretched out an arm as if offering himself as a pillow. I curled up, facing away from him, my blanket still wrapped around me. His side leaned against me, his warmth electric.

"I'll keep you secure," he said, and his words had me exhaling a long breath.

Aside from having no other option of escape, part of me trusted him. He'd saved me from the wolves, brought me into this cave, kept me warm. Why would he want to harm me after that? Despite everything, I had to believe Oryn wasn't a bad person, but someone with too much compassion who wore spiked thorns for armor. I understood his approach to life: stay in charge, protect others, never let anyone get close. That way, he wouldn't get hurt again. I'd been there. Except, he was fooling himself. His family... the pack was already in his heart, whether or not he admitted it. Just the way he spoke about them screamed "father figure." And that was a man, in my eyes, who would keep his promise and keep me safe.

"Oryn," I began, my eyelids growing heavy. I closed them as the weight of the day dragged me down. "Thank you. I wish I could say if you came to Terra, someone would offer you the same protection, but I can't. If it were me, I would risk everything to help you."

A long pause passed and heaviness wove through my limbs as my mind drifted toward sleep.

Oryn's whisper glided into my thoughts. "What have you done to me?"

* * *

THE TOUCH of a light breeze tickled my legs, bringing with it a chill. I hugged a warm pillow, inhaling its musky scent, adoring the smell. It reminded me of Oryn, and a blaze pooled deep in my gut at the memory of how gorgeous he was.

When fingers brushed through my hair, I flipped open my eyes to find myself draped over him, pressed against him naked. A dim light from the fire threw shadows across his face and chest, and it remained dark outside.

"Morning," he said in his husky voice.

"Sorry for sleeping on you." I retreated, patting the covered floor behind me to find we both rested on my blanket.

"No problem. The fire's almost out, and it's cold this early." His arm remained on my back, massaging me, easing my earlier panic.

"How long have you been awake?" I asked.

He lay there, his other arm behind his head, reflecting the perfect epitome of a fantasy man. Layers of muscles, a chest so wide I could snooze on it... which I had... and... *Don't stare down his body whatever you do.*

Chewing on my lower lip, I kept his gaze. *Hooray for me.*

"I woke early, but I didn't want to wake you."

"So you held me?"

Those sexy blue eyes smiled, staring at me with all the kinds of intentions that had me picturing myself leaning over and kissing him. Those were the kinds of uncontrollable longings that had led me to have sex with Nero instead of finding a way home.

Still, my pulse skipped a beat. "I bet girls throw themselves at you all the time."

He turned onto his side to face me. "Would you expect anything else?"

I rolled my eyes and laughed. "That's right. You're the alpha and have your pick of partners."

"Something like that." He touched my shoulder. "But you're different."

"Well, yeah. I *am* human."

"No." He skimmed his fingers over my shoulder and to just above my heart. "Something in there makes you unlike anyone I've encountered. My wolf calls to you, and he's never claimed someone before."

Nero had said similar words. Was it my ability somehow messing with their wolves? But then, why did the urge to get closer to them intensify?

"Is that your pick-up line?" *Heavens*, I sounded dorky. Then again, I wasn't sure where to look. I lay naked with a man with a dark side and was trapped in the cave. No wonder all kinds of crazy poured from my mouth.

"I always speak my mind."

"Oh." So he thought we were mates? Didn't Nero hint at the same thing? Which seemed impossible considering I wasn't a wolf, and how in the world was I supposed to be a match for them both? Nope. The strangeness just kept on swirling out of control, not to mention my libido.

"I'd tell you the truth," he began. "Like how sexy your breasts are." His caress dipped down between the valley of my boobs and trailed a finger around the outer edges of my areola. "So pink and perky."

I gasped for air as he pinched a tight nipple, and I moaned as my pulse skyrocketed and the desperate urge for release tore through me.

"I could watch you all day."

Brushing his hand away, I said, "Are you always so forward?"

"I'm curious to discover why my wolf is whispering in my ear to take you, to eat you out, and claim you as ours."

I rocked on the spot at his admittance, and was it bad that I loved it? A deep, commanding voice inside me demanded I give myself to him, let him claim me, and for me to melt under him. The right decision was to insist we leave. But damn, curiosity burned a hole through my chest. I'd never had a man speak in such ways to me, yet in two days, I'd experienced it twice. Maybe this whole experience was an illusion. I'd hit my head and lay unconscious somewhere in the woods.

Despite my better judgment, my attraction for him stirred, craving him as if my life depended on it. Nero had mentioned that once a wolf made love with someone their wolf claimed, they were mates for life, but surely that didn't apply here. Or did Oryn see me as an easy score after seeing Nero and me hook up?

"I never kiss strange men. But something about Nero and you is pulling me like a magnet. And I don't get it, or how messed up it is that I want you both. Please don't hate me for that." I shyly looked away, burning up from the inside out. I'd never thought I'd say such things to anyone, but there they were. Geez, was I going to react this way with all wolf shifters I met?

"It's okay." He touched my chin and lifted my head to face him. "Hunters can have multiple partners if their wolves connect. Nero's my wolf brother and if both our wolves desire you, I'd be honored."

My head spun, unsure what he was saying. They would share me? Heavens, this had to be a dream if two gorgeous hunks agreed to both be with me. I'd take one, but two... No, someone had pulled a practical joke on me and I placed my bets on Bee. "I'm not a wolf. This can't be happening. My touch affects you both." It was the most reasonable explanation.

He placed my palm to his chest. "My wolf is the matchmaker and selects my soulmate."

"This can't be." I swallowed hard, considering the possibility this was true, me with two different men who were shifters.

"Such a shame," he said.

"What is?" I whispered.

"That you doubt our connection without knowing how well I could treat you. How well I can tease your sweet blossom until you come for me. How much you'll love screaming my name."

I gasped because no one had ever spoken to me with such dirty words.

He pulled me closer, our bodies against each other, and his hand squeezed my ass. He growled quietly in my ear. "I can smell your arousal. I know you want me." Without another word, he kissed me, and a shiver caught between my legs.

My pulse raced. I didn't care to understand our attraction, not when I'd just tasted his lips and heat roared through me. So I kissed him hard, pressing myself against him, needing him, inhaling him. Everything in my head might have screamed to backpedal from this slippery road, but my body and soul demanded I take Oryn and make him mine.

CHAPTER 10

Oryn kissed me with the passion of a starved wolf. Fast, hard, and demanding. My pulse galloped. Nothing compared to having him kiss me. Yep, I'd become a horny beast, and if I ever got home, Bee would demand I spill every dirty detail.

His mouth trailed down my neck, licking me all the way down to my breasts, flicking my nipples. I lay on my back on the blankets, thrumming with excitement. His fingers swirled down my waist and skipped over to an inner thigh. I winced as a cool breeze brushed against my burning sex.

"Tell me what you want me to do," he breathed against my breast before taking it into his mouth, suckling me.

I writhed, unable to find my words when his touch skimmed my inner thigh… so close, yet too far.

"Please, Oryn." The words rushed, and I drowned under his seductive spell.

"Say it." He inched down my body, leaving a trail of nibbles along my stomach, positioning himself between my legs, nudging them open.

My breath caught in my chest, and I chewed on my lower

lip. "I…" My voice faded, my face burning with uncertainty from voicing what I wanted.

He blew a warm breath of air across the apex of my legs, and I squirmed as the desperation to have him intensified.

"Fuck, your honeyed pussy looks delicious." He flicked the inside of my thigh and gently gnawed on my flesh.

I raised myself on my elbows and watched him between my legs, his gaze on my privates. The image alone had me pulsing. I swallowed past the thickness in my throat. "Take me."

"No, no. Give it to me. Foul-mouthed and sexy."

"I don't know how," I whispered.

He winked at me and dipped closer, his tongue curling over my clit. "Yes, you do."

I convulsed, my core tightening.

He ran a finger down my slit. "So sticky and wet."

Heavens, who was this man? I collapsed on my back, driving aside my worries and the part of me that made me cringe at using swear words. I trembled with need and that same inner voice demanded I let Oryn pull me into his darkest fantasy. I didn't care that I'd now slept with two different men in two days, that I might burn in the underworld for eternity, that I'd never be able to tell a soul without dying of embarrassment.

Another tiny flick, and I arched my back, mewling. "Hell. Eat me. Pleasure me. Please, just tongue fuck me already." My face burned with embarrassment.

He laughed. "That's my girl." His lips clasped around my privates, sucking. I moaned, forgetting my shyness. His tongue was divine, while his fingers teased my opening.

I clutched the blankets in my fists, losing myself. Right now, I crumbled beneath Oryn's attention. A shudder traveled through me, sizzling me from the inside out. Each lick left me panting.

He lapped at my inner lips, pulling at them. When I glanced down my body, he winked with the most devilish expression.

"Oh, my."

"Don't make me stop. Swear for me."

Catching my breath seemed an impossibility. "You're killing me."

He lifted himself, licking glistening lips and lightly slapping my hip. "Roll over and show me that ass."

Every inch of me smoldered, and the inferno between my thighs fell under the control of this captivating man. "I need you."

He smirked that sexy grin. "Turn over for me and try again."

What was it about these wolves and their dominating ways...? Damn if it didn't twist my libido into a knot. Right now, I'd do anything he asked, so I flipped over onto my stomach, drowning in heat.

Oryn spread my legs and positioned himself there, his hands gliding over my butt cheeks, prying them open. "Girl, you're so fucking beautiful."

I started to twist around, but he laid his body over mine, forcing me back down. His breath was in my ear, warming across my cheek.

"I'm going to fuck that sweet blossom of yours and you're going to scream my name." His cock twitched against my butt.

"Shit, Oryn."

His words melted me. I'd always stayed in control, owned my own destiny. But having someone so strong and controlling unraveled me. I craved him, ached for this scorching caress. And I couldn't wait.

"Fuck my pussy and make me hurt."

"Love hearing filthy words from your mouth," he said and

he slid down my body, kissing along my spine, taking mock bites out of my butt cheeks.

I gasped.

He pulled up my hips, and my ass perched in the air. When his tip pressed against my entrance, I tilted my pelvis to meet him.

"That's my girl." Gripping my hips, he pushed into me, stretching me.

I cried out as he drove deeper, and I loved every goddamn moment.

"You're mine forever," he snarled.

He thrust in and out so fast, I lost my breath with each plunge. Harder, stronger, and filling me completely.

I squirmed, unable to stop as the sensation rubbed my insides. Logic flew out the window when all I focused on was our point of contact, the slapping sounds, his grunts.

His fingers slid down my crack and teased my ass. A first for me, yet it had me aching for more but, then again, everything about him drove me wild. When a finger entered my rear, I screamed as a wave crashed through me.

"Come for me."

I convulsed, gripping the blanket, gasping for air as an orgasm rocked me. "Fuuuuuck."

Oryn roared, his grip digging into my flesh as he stiffened, exploding inside me. We stayed like that, heaving for breath, coated in sweat. And for those few moments, the world felt perfect, and I didn't want a single thing to change.

When he pulled out, I collapsed on the blanket and he did the same alongside me, collecting me into his arms. We were face-to-face, so close I could kiss his nose.

"Incredi—"

His lips crushed against mine. "You have the sweetest pussy."

I blushed. Crazy considering what he'd just done to me,

but I fell for him hard. Despite his dirty words and my lust-fogged brain, I was lost to this man. With my head cradled against his chest, I listened to his heartbeat, pounding, matching my own. In his hold, I remained protected, adored, as if nothing in the world could touch me. I let myself believe the fantasy of being with two amazing shifters, telling myself they weren't hunters, that our races didn't hate each other, and that we could make it work.

As much as all that logical crap swished through my brain, I couldn't deny the cold hard truth of how I felt. Which shouldn't have been happening. Even with Oryn admitting they practiced sharing mates, this was foreign to me—strange, yet tantalizing.

* * *

"Wake up," Oryn whispered in my ear. "We need to go."

Grogginess grasped my mind, but I sat up. The fire was out, and soft orange rays pierced the waterfall from outside. Morning. Oryn took my hand and helped me to my feet, the blanket cascading off my body and around my feet.

"Time to go, gorgeous." He kissed my brow and guided me to the lagoon's edge.

"Can I take a blanket?" I asked, not quite ready to parade around naked. The shifters might have found it easy... I didn't, but Oryn wasn't waiting and had already stepped into the water and turned to me. "Come to me, I'll carry you across. It'll be faster."

I gave no argument, as I was certain if I traveled on my own, the crashing fall would drive me underwater, and I'd already almost drowned yesterday. I dropped the blanket and stepped into the lagoon, iciness spiking up my legs. "It's freezing."

Oryn raised a brow, as if such protests were beneath him,

but, without a word, he lifted me in his arms as if I were a damsel in distress. Well, maybe I was, and I wasn't protesting.

"This will be fast. I promise." And we were off.

I held on as he rushed through the downpour crushing us. Within moments, we were out. He'd bulldozed through the foamy water that had splashed over my chest and hardened my nipples. "You can put me down here," I said. "Just need a smidgen of private time, please."

He leered at me, blank at first, then his eyes widened in realization. "Don't be long." Once out of the river, he studied the forest and, thank goodness, kept his back to me.

In haste, I relieved myself and cleaned up, never in a trillion years imagining I'd pee out in public in front of a hunk. Yep, that was what my life had come to.

By the time I climbed out and joined Oryn, he took my hand in his and we marched toward the woods. I adored his overprotectiveness; something about it left me giddy. The morning sun beat on my shoulders, warming me, and birds sang in the distance. There wasn't any sign of wolves. Perfect. The faint waft of pine floated on the breeze. If I didn't know better, I could have mistaken the place for Terra.

Oryn sniffed the air and swung toward the upward slope of a ledge, alongside the forest on one side and the river on the other. We stayed to the grass, as opposed to foliage and rocks… those things would tear up my feet.

"Thank you," I said.

He stopped and glanced around before looking down at me. "We need to keep quiet and move fast," he said. "But out of curiosity, are you thanking me for sex or keeping you safe?" He smirked.

I nudged his arm. "You'll never know. Now let's move."

With a nod, he moved forward, tugging me alongside. Halfway up, a howl rang in the distance, and I flinched, bumping into Oryn's side.

We rushed up, and panic gripped my chest. I glanced over my shoulder, expecting to see wolves chasing us. That was all we needed. Our options were to run deeper into the woods, where we'd be easy prey, or jump off the cliff into the river. Neither option uncoiled the growing dread in my gut.

A grunt burst from deep in the pine forest.

We moved faster, running now. I clasped an arm against my breasts, their bouncing movement distracting me—and, clearly, Oryn, who kept glancing my way.

Almost at the top, he quickened his steps. My breaths grew short and raspy. Wind tugged my hair, and, despite the chill, sweat dripped down my back.

Up ahead, twenty feet away, two brown wolves emerged from the forest. One growled, the fur on its neck standing on end.

Oryn halted, one arm pushing me behind him. "Run to the house when I say *go*."

My gut dropped to my feet and my pulse skipped a beat.

When a howl came from behind us, I jerked around and faced another dark wolf skulking closer out of the woods.

I shuddered as a strangled cry fell from my lips.

CHAPTER 11

"*W*here do we go now?" My words rushed out, and I clasped on to Oryn's arm. I hated this vulnerability thing and being naked wasn't helping in the slightest.

Oryn and I pressed together, back to back, and an icy wind curled through my hair. Three wolves surrounded us, the forest on one side and a sharp cliff overlooking the river on the other.

Already I felt Oryn's skin twitching. While he might fight one or two, another wolf was bound to get me. Why did everything in the Den try to kill me at every turn? I wasn't sure I'd ever feel safe going through a forest alone again if I ever got out of this alive.

A charge zipped up my spine, and I snapped around. Oryn had transformed into his wolf form... the sensation tingling along my flesh akin to how my ability affected me. Did the shifters use enchantment to transform? It might explain why both Oryn and Nero had responded to my touch.

He nudged his head against my thigh. With the woods at

my rear, I swung my attention left and right to the wolves on either side of us. My breaths sped, and I scanned the ground for something to defend myself with… twigs and pebbles. *Great.*

With a sudden grunt, the animal on my right charged. I recoiled.

Oryn pivoted and tore at the foe, leaving me with the other two beasts inching toward me.

My mouth dried, and I couldn't swallow. Leaping off the cliff sounded more enticing by the moment. Oryn and his attacker rolled across the grass, one of them yelping.

"Oryn!"

I backpedaled.

A snarl erupted behind me.

Every hair on my body stood on end. *Heavens, please just this once, give me a break.*

I gawked at the two approaching fiends. Behind me, an enormous white wolf crouched between two overgrown shrubs. My heart drummed so loud, I trembled.

But when the newcomer tilted his head in my direction and pointed his chin behind him, a move I'd have expected someone to use when telling me to move out of the way, reality smacked into me. The white fur, not striking when he'd snuck up on me.

Nero!

A cry of happiness gurgled on my throat.

The tapping of paws on soil reached me. I spun as the two wolves charged for me, fur bristled, fangs exposed.

Shuddering, I jerked around and darted past Nero and into the woodland.

Growls exploded behind me.

I spun, fists raised.

Nero fought both wolves, biting down on the back of one

animal's neck, the other he kicked in the face with a leg. The second one leaped toward him, and Nero yelped.

My heart dropped to my feet, and before I could think straight, I was running to him.

But a black blur zipped from the left and crash-tackled the animal, freeing Nero. It was Oryn, and now both jumped into the brawl, driving the attacking hounds out of the woods. The one from under Nero whined and retreated, scrambling away.

Oryn had his wolf pinned down, his jaws latched on the animal's throat. He released a thunderous growl and looked my way.

Unable to move, I wasn't catching up with what he was doing or implying. When the wolf flinched, it hit me… Our discussion in the cave about him capturing a wolf to discover if my ability could aid them to transform back.

I rushed closer and crouched behind the animal, then called to my power. The spark of energy flared, and I laid a hand on his furry rump.

We waited.

Nothing, so I rubbed my hand across the fur.

The white energy lines sparked. *Yes.*

Except they curved upward from my fingertips and shot toward Oryn's face. At once, he lurched backward, and already his body was shifting back into a human.

"No!" I retreated from the wild wolf scrambling onto his paws, facing me, unleashing a snarl.

Nero flew between us in a flash, snapping his teeth at the creature. The wolf bolted away.

I collapsed against a tree and my legs wobbled from the dread in my veins. Nero sniffed at Oryn, who was on hands and knees, fur vanishing, his limbs elongating.

"Sorry, Oryn," I said.

Nero shook himself and already his snout withdrew,

while his body grew in size. The sound of bones cracking coupled the lengthening of the spine as his curved body straightened.

I'd never seen a wolf transform. No one in Terra had or truly understood how they changed, but in witnessing the amazing event, I gawked at the beauty of how their bodies shape-shifted with such ease.

Gone were the wolves, replaced by two perfect specimens of men, naked, and climbing to their feet.

Oryn stood taller and wider than Nero, making me melt, but Nero's boyish charm and his wink had the fire in my libido awakening. They were perfect in their own way. But how was I attracted to both equally?

Fresh scratches and bite marks covered their arms and shoulders, yet nothing looked life-threatening.

Nero strode toward me, and my pulse skyrocketed. His hand glided across my back, drawing me against him. "Should have figured Oryn was looking out for you. Been searching for you all night. Had me worried sick."

I glanced up at him, the concern spiraling in his eyes. "You did that for me?"

"Little lamb, I'd scour the world to find you." He held me tight. "And I adore this whole 'going naked' look. Suits you, sexy girl."

I blushed and pressed up against him.

Oryn approached, and Nero clapped his friend on the shoulder before saying, "How'd you break out of your wolf form?"

"Sharlot has a magical touch." He approached me, a hand sliding to my butt, and I met his gaze, the sexiness in his eyes.

Nero looked at me, mouthing, "Sharlot," then he smirked.

I rolled my eyes and smiled right back.

Heavens, was this happening? Me with two hunks? "So." I swallowed past my thickening throat. "This thing...

between us three." I racked my brain for the right word, but nothing came to mind when I still wasn't sure what to make of it myself, except I didn't want to be apart from either man.

"We return to the house first." Oryn's deep tone returned, the authoritarian one where he took control.

"Of course. If I never confront an attacking wolf again, I'll have a very happy life," I said.

We moved in unison, the men flanking me, fast-walking through the forest, my feet aching from the sharp rocks and twigs. But other emotions distracted me with the newfound excitement that two men stared at me as if I were candy! Me! The girl who couldn't get a date to the annual town dance, while Bee'd had eight suitors.

But reality checked in about how I'd leave the Den, how I might lose my men, and how the priestess had probably set guards to watch my store. The earlier joy deflated, replaced with a cramping beneath my breastbone. What was I supposed to do?

Once we reached the house and Nero had locked the door, we plonked down on chairs, me between the men, staring at an empty table. I hugged myself and Oryn brought me a blanket, which I wore like a strapless dress, and that small modesty had me relaxing into my seat.

"We don't have clothes on hand," he said. "We don't wear them, and I preferred you better naked."

I laughed. "This is perfect, thanks. Anyway, my touch didn't work on that wild wolf," I blurted out to avoid talking about the obvious elephant in the room—me having had sex with two wolf shifters in as many days and now we all sat together as if that was okay. Sure, Oryn said he was fine with it, but what about Nero?

Oryn nodded and ran his fingers through his shoulder-length hair, worry crammed behind his gaze.

I sighed. "My ability only works on you two." I shifted in my seat, looking from one man to the other.

"Well, this is a first for me, on so many levels. And I don't understand what I'm feeling, but..." How to put this? "I like you both." This was the weirdest conversation ever and not one I'd ever imagined myself having.

Nero laughed and caressed my thigh, sending tingles upward. "Why do you sound so worried? My wolf has claimed you. When you left, I couldn't think of anything else but finding you, so I know we're meant to be. Besides, I smelled Oryn on you the moment I found you in the forest... his wolf claimed you as well, right?"

I nodded, dropping my gaze.

Oryn placed a hand on my other thigh. "It's okay. Having multiple mates is normal for hunters."

I stared from one man to the other. "So you're okay with this? Because I'm freaking out."

The men exchanged a knowing look, and it comforted me to know they shared such a trusting bond, stirring a desire to give in to what I wanted and forget my concerns.

Nero burst out laughing, while Oryn leaned in and kissed me, his warmth adding fuel to the blaze. "You're safe and ours," he said. "You need not fret."

"We are wolf brothers," Nero began, "and I would risk my life to save Oryn's, along with yours. We're bound, the three of us."

Okay, that earlier excitement returned three-fold because technically I had two boyfriends, right? Oh geez, Bee would bombard me with rude jokes if she heard about this.

"So how does this work? Are we now dating?"

Nero ruffled my hair and closed in for a kiss, soft and passionate. "You're too adorable. But when a wolf selects a mate, it's for life. We're way past dating, little lamb."

I sat there, trying to process his words. For life! That

terrified me because this whole mating thing was moving too fast. They were shifters, so this might be natural to them, but for me... Each breath sped. Who was I kidding? Just thinking of going to Terra and leaving the men behind had an invisible vise constricting my heart.

"What if...?" I began. "What if what we're feeling is my ability tampering with your wolves? Confusing them?"

Oryn plucked a twig out of my hair and drew me backward against him. He wrapped an arm across my shoulders and kissed my head. "In the cave, our connection shook through me, my wolf awakening, opening up to welcome you to our bonding. This is real, unlike anything I've ever felt, and everything inside me demands you are mine. I have no doubts. Doesn't matter if you're not one of us."

Nero lifted my feet and placed them on his lap, rubbing my soles in a way that had me softening. Now, this I could get used to.

"Sweet lamb, when you vanished, and I searched for you, I swore I'd go insane if I didn't find you. Losing you isn't even a consideration. You are also mine."

No response came to mind, only the whirling tornado of a million questions, from me desiring shifters, to whether I had to move to a new home, and even if their packs would accept me... heavens, those were insane thoughts and it hurt my brain trying to make sense of them. Too much had happened too quickly, and my spinning mind hadn't caught up yet. Sure, I knew without a shadow of a doubt that my attraction toward them owned me. And their smallest caress undid me. But I ought to get to know them better, and such a commitment was huge.

Grandma had always told me to never move too fast with a man, but when I found him, I'd sense it. And that was Nero and Oryn for me. Unable to picture myself living without them. But how could I experience such devotion in such a short time?

I pushed my feet off Nero's lap and rose out of Oryn's arms. Both men stared at me, and I yearned for nothing more than to remain in their embraces, talking about setting up home in the woods, and forgetting everything else. Learn Nero's tricks in the kitchen, Oryn's tracking skills. But what about my shop? Friends? People I assisted with herbs?

Were the walls closing in around me? Going outside for fresh air was out of the question with those vicious wolves prowling around, and as much as I yearned to ask to be taken home, I refused to leave their side. Talk about being a walking contradiction.

My thoughts flew to Dagen and how I hadn't even given him a thought since arriving back. I'd harmed him, and it was my responsibility to help him.

"I'll check on Dagen." I didn't wait for a response but sprinted out of the room and down the dark hallway toward the shifter I'd injured and who needed my attention. Yep, that was what I'd do. Focus on healing him and try to sort out the mess in my head before I did something mental like agree to move in with them right away.

CHAPTER 12

"Well," I began as I leaned over Dagen, who remained unconscious, "so many things have happened since we last chatted. Like insane things that might make you laugh out loud. Can you believe I slept with both your friends, and now they've claimed me as their own?" I shook my head. "Told you it was crazy stuff." Though based on what Nero had told me about shifters having multiple partners, Dagen most likely had a harem of his own.

While in a coma, he couldn't hear me, and a sense of relief flooded me at voicing that out loud and not having anyone judge me. Though part of me felt as if I ought to be judged. Damn, anyone in Terra would think I'd grown devil horns if they got wind of what I'd been up to.

"And the strange thing is that I can't stop thinking about them both." I combed Dagen's hair with my fingers, pushing the longer strands off his face. "It's as if they've hypnotized me, yet my eyes are wide open, and I can't bring myself to walk away. That's weird, right?" I sighed and glanced down at the wolf shifter with pale cheeks, yet his stubble had thickened. He was incredibly handsome.

"Just between us, if you were awake, I'd love to taste your lips." I blushed the moment the words left my mouth, and I plopped down on the seat next to the bed. Goddess, what had become of me? Was any wolf shifter safe around my libido?

Control—I had zilch.

His bandages were crisp and white where before blood had stained them. Nero must have changed them. I zigzagged my thumb down his arm between two bandages, and a faint charge sparked across his flesh.

That hadn't happened before, and excitement had me jolting to my feet. Was this a sign that my power could awaken him? I ripped off the damn fabrics across his chest and arms, then placed both palms flat across his perfect pecs. Every molecule in my body buzzed as I concentrated on driving the strength within me down my arms, picturing the flow of power racing into Dagen.

A spider web of blue static laced outward from my fingertips, crawling up and over his collarbone, up his neck and across his jawline.

"Please wake up, Dagen."

My flesh tingled.

Sparks crackled across his torso, except he didn't stir. When I had touched Oryn in his wolf form, he'd shuddered right away. So why not Dagen? Perhaps it was the whole mate thing the men had mentioned. They responded because we were apparently meant to be together. Not that I was looking to add another man to my growing harem. Geez, I sounded crazy. But what if he never woke up?

Guilt wormed through my chest as he lay there, yet I'd seen how quickly Oryn had recovered after his wolf fights.

"Why aren't you waking up or healing?" Wolfsbane had definitely affected him through my contaminated citrus spray. The fact that he hadn't died meant only a small portion of the toxin had gotten into his system. But still, I'd done everything I could for him. I wasn't sure any of my herbs would help, either.

I paced to the door and back. Grandma had once explained charcoal was her go-to solution for poisoning if nothing else worked. I could dribble some down his throat, but I didn't want him choking to death.

"What am I going to do?" I chewed on my cheek, remembering how my fingers had sparked when I'd traced his bicep while having hot and heavy thoughts about him. Maybe the reason Oryn responded to my touch the same as Nero was because my intent had been sexual in nature.

Staring at Dagen, the blanket covering his hips, I had no intention of groping him again, but my gaze lingered on his lips. "I'm going to try something, but don't freak out." I laughed at myself and how insane I sounded.

But I pushed those thoughts aside and refocused instead on the perfect curves of his cheekbones, the honey-colored stubble over a strong jaw. His neck had layers of muscles to rival Oryn.

I leaned closer. "Please, Dagen. If you can hear me, wake up. I'm sorry for hurting you."

With my lips brushing his dry ones, I exhaled, letting myself soften.

Static snapped between us and thrust me backward. I gasped, but strong hands grasped my wrists, drawing me forward once again. My legs tangled beneath me and I fell across the bed.

Dagen's fingers dug into my flesh and his eyes flipped open, revealing the most incredible clear emerald irises.

I stumbled back to my feet, my blanket unraveling from around me and cascading down my naked body.

A growl rolled through his chest, and while I should have been ecstatic he was conscious, the hunger in his gaze terrified me. It reminded me of the wolves outside, the ones that wanted to kill me.

"Dagen, let me go!" I pulled against him, reaching down for the blanket, but he only tightened his grasp, and dread slithered up my spine.

"Who are you?" His darkened baritone carried a gravelly tinge and he snatched the blanket from my grip, tossing it across the room.

"I'm Scarlet." I twisted toward the door and called out, "Nero, Oryn, I could use some help. Dagen's awake!"

But he was on his feet in two seconds, bandages falling off his strong legs. His clutch never eased. He drove me backward, his height towering over me.

"Why is a human in our home?"

"Please." I trembled, convinced Dagen would tear me apart in under a second.

"Oryn!" I yelled. "Nero!"

Dagen glanced over his shoulder and sniffed the air. "Looks like it's just us two, alone in the house."

"What? No, they're in the kitchen. They'll tell you the truth. I'm here to heal you."

He tsked, and a grin split his mouth, revealing white teeth. "You attacked me in the woods. And you expect me to believe you've now saved me? I might still be groggy, but I'm no fool."

The ache in my arms radiated from his grip, and, hell, if this was him groggy, would he have torn my heart out of my chest if fully alert?

"You're not too bright," I blurted out, not sure what to say next. At once, I regretted my sudden confidence. Only to have it deflate under his piercing gaze. But those green eyes... I could drown in them, get lost for eternity, die in his arms as long as I stayed here. As insane as my thoughts were, my body shivered with anticipation.

"I will not hurt you," I insisted.

The pain in my arms eased from his loosened grasp, and I raised a hand, touching his chest, hoping it might connect us, help him calm down.

Energy buzzed from my fingertips, spreading outward as it had earlier.

His body trembled, and he stumbled backward, his gaze flittering across his torso. Narrowing eyes fastened on me, and a snarl rolled from his throat. His shoulders curled forward. Just as I'd seen Oryn do in the cave when he lost control.

My breaths were in a marathon and my lungs were losing the battle. I sidestepped along the wall, every inch of me shivering.

"What did you do?" he barked.

"Please don't hurt me." I spied the door about five feet away.

He shook his head and kept whacking the heel of his hand into his temple.

Escape was my only chance of survival. And where the hell were the men? Yep, they'd find their friend conscious and me dead. A choked cry fell from my lips.

Bastards! Huh, I only seemed to swear when facing death.

I turned and sprinted, but he moved so fast, my vision blurred. He shoved me against the wall and pushed me by the shoulder to face away from him. His hot breath blew through my hair as he whispered in my ear, "So you want to taste my lips again?"

"Wait, what?" An attempt to turn was impossible as he pushed himself against my back, squishing me. "If you heard me while you were out of it, then you know I'm not the enemy here."

"Maybe, but what concerns me right now is why your scent is fogging my head. Why some of your thoughts fill my mind. Why all I can think about is me fucking you. Except, I don't do humans!"

With my cheek pressed to the wall, and his hands crawling up the sides of my body, I raised my voice to show him I wasn't a pushover. "Arrogant much? And I don't do shifters, either." Damn, I was the worst liar in the world.

His laughter covered me in pinpricks, the kind that dove south and curled in the apex of my legs. Heavens! This hunter could snap my neck off, and here I suffocated in heat.

"That's why my friends' scents are all over you." He pulled the hair off the side of my face, his stubble grazing my cheek as he responded, "Shall we try again? What did you cast on me?"

"H-Healed you. But that's okay, you need not thank me. Heavens forbid you show gratitude."

He stiffened for a moment but didn't back away. "And the magic from your touch? Did you cast a delusion spell so I'd fall victim to your seduction until you escaped? Is that what you've done to my wolf brothers?"

My mouth opened, but nothing came out at first. I hadn't once considered that an option, but it warranted considera-tion. "I mean you no harm."

"I can smell your lies from your perspiration."

"Because you're squashing me and I can hardly breathe, you psycho shifter!"

"Hunter," he growled in my ear.

"Okay, hunter. Now let me go," I yelled.

When his weight eased away, I turned around, but he remained there, arms on the wall on either side of me, glaring down at me.

His mouth slammed against mine, hard and unforgiving. His tongue pushed into my mouth, tangling with mine, and as much I wanted to knee him in the balls, something was happening.

A euphoric pulse coiled deep in my gut, diving deeper, and my heartbeat was a bomb in my chest, ready to detonate. I hated his forcefulness but couldn't get enough at the same time. What was wrong with me? His hardness pressed against my stomach, and I trembled with the need to reach down and feel him.

"Yes, grab me there," he whispered against my mouth.

What? Hadn't I just thought that?

He kissed me again, stealing my words but not my thoughts. Had he read my mind? This was too much, and I thrust my hands against his chest, pushing him off me.

He licked his lips. "I don't know how, but you're in my head. I keep receiving snippets of your thoughts, words here and there."

"How?" I couldn't hear a thing aside from my pulse banging in my skull like a drum.

"You tell me," he began. "You're the magic user. And while you're at it, explain why you're enchanting me into craving you when I would never want a vile human."

The earlier excitement dwindled and left me feeling dirty and empty. I'd been called many things in my life, but never "vile," and not by someone I'd just kissed.

CHAPTER 13

"*V*ile? Please." I lifted my chin to make myself look bigger compared to this six-foot-two man wearing a wry expression. "I could call you worse things for threatening me after I cured you."

"You put me in that situation," Dagen boomed.

Anger fueled my response because I was getting sick of this wolf dominance shit. "You attacked me in the woods!"

His furrowed brow softened.

"Okay, maybe not *attacked*, but how was I supposed to know any different when three wolves came at me?"

His chest lifted and fell quickly, as if his patience was fading fast.

"I was defending myself. So why are you mad at me?" I glanced toward the open door. Surely, Nero or Oryn would come any moment and discover their grumpy friend was awake.

"Because humans aren't supposed to be here. You kill anything that moves, anything you don't understand."

I folded my arms across my chest. "Is that right, Mr. Stereotyping Everyone? Does that mean I can assume all wolves are sadistic monsters who'll kill anyone without a hint of mercy, like the ones outside?"

He swiveled his jaw from side to side, making a clicking sound. "That's an abnormality in Oryn's pack."

Hypocrite. "And whatever human got you so riled up in the past was a one-off and in no way reflects who I am."

The corner of his upper lip curled upward, and a guttural snarl rolled through his chest. Okay, he didn't appreciate being proved wrong.

"You clearly know nothing about what your kind is capable of, the countless wolves they've hunted and skinned alive."

I swallowed the rock in my throat. Those atrocities had happened decades ago.

"Yes, but the barbaric acts are still happening," he replied out loud to my thoughts. "Just last full moon, we discovered two wolves butchered on our land, with cuts from human blades."

"Stop reading my mind." I didn't want to believe what he said, even though the priestess loathed wolves, so what if…?

"Your priestess has a lot to pay for."

I picked at a hangnail, unable to defend her when I'd seen a dark side to her and no way in the underworld would I assume she was all butterflies and flowers. But was she slaughtering wolves? It went against the peace pact that every realm had made when they'd split up centuries ago. Why would she risk a death penalty? The only rule that kept territories in check was to murder no one.

"She'll be held accountable like anyone else," he growled.

"If you can prove she did it to the councils in each realm," I said, unable to believe I was attempting to defend her, but the rules were clear.

"Oryn has seen the priestess watching her guards murder

a wolf. Death is coming for her." His tone darkened, and I didn't have a single doubt he meant every word.

I wasn't sure how to feel, because I didn't support murder, but if what he said was true, then the priestess needed to step down from her position or be imprisoned in one of her dungeons.

"So what now?" I broke the silence.

When I turned toward the door, figuring this was my getaway, Dagen snatched my wrist and forced me to face him. "We're not done here. Tell me about your magic and how you're controlling me."

I wrinkled my nose and huffed. "If I could command you, would I let you scare me? Is that how you manage your pack? With fear?"

His grip tightened. "You don't know anything about me."

This whole dual personality within me—flipping from craving Dagen to getting pissed off at him—was getting on my nerves. I ripped my hand free.

"Look, I get it, you hate me, fine. That doesn't mean I'll let you treat me like crap." I spun on my heels, grabbed the blanket a few feet away, and marched out the door and into the corridor.

Yep, "arrogant" and "hypocritical" perfectly suited Dagen. Should have left him unconscious. He had been much nicer then. And I didn't care if he heard me think that.

I pushed open the kitchen door and found the room empty. Where were the men? The door to the outside remained shut, so I retreated and checked the living room with the fireplace, finding it also bare. With a quick check of the house, I still couldn't track them down.

"Told you we were alone." Dagen leaned against the door-frame to the bedroom, standing there stark naked, a silhouette of candlelight glowing around him.

"You want a gold star for being right?"

He chuckled, and I turned away before I threw something at him. How could I hate and crave someone at the same time? Was that even possible?

I stormed into the kitchen and closed myself in, leaning my back against the door. Dagen drove me up the wall with fury, with desire. Standing there all naked with his enormous... I gasped. How dare he call me vile?

"I can still hear you," he yelled from somewhere in the house.

"Agh... If you're in my head, you'll know I'm not evil," I screamed, anything to stop the memories swirling out of control, remembering his hardness, the hunger of his lips, and heavens, I so wanted more.

He laughed.

I grunted and paced across the kitchen. "Blue skies, birds, herbs. Arrowroot, chamomile, feverfew, lavender, marigold." I chanted them in my head.

When the outside door slapped open, I jumped, and my breath wedged in my throat.

Nero and Oryn poured inside and kicked the door closed after them. A new scratch ran down Oryn's arm, and a few marred Nero's chest, but the blood had already coagulated.

"What happened? Where did you go? Dagen is insane, and he could have killed me." My words merged into one huge sentence as my breaths sped.

"Dagen's awake?" Oryn asked as he rushed out into the hall.

Nero's gaze followed him, but he approached me and guided a lock behind my ears. "Did he hurt you, little lamb?"

I shook my head. "But he wanted to."

"He never would. That's just how he is. Growl first, then get to know someone."

Nero pulled me into his arms, and I molded against his chest. "We scoured fifty acres around the house in every direction to see how many of Oryn's wolves were near. Close to twenty. We frightened a few off."

That simple notion had me pressing closer, and yet my focus persisted on my earlier encounter in the bedroom. "Dagen hates humans, doesn't he?" I glanced up to Nero. "And why are there so many wolves so close to the house? If they broke in, they'd easily overpower the three of you."

"You worry too much. This house is strong and no wolf is getting inside. With regards to Dagen, he's had unfortunate run-ins with humans, and it left him very suspicious toward your kind."

I chewed on my cheek. *Wonderful.* No matter what my hormones insisted, I would keep my distance from him. And maybe my ability had impacted this whole mating thing, otherwise why else would I consider Dagen anything but an enemy? *Oh, crap!* No more thinking like that while he tapped into my thoughts. Basil, rosemary, chicken soup.

My stomach rumbled.

"You hungry?" Nero asked.

"I could eat a horse right now."

He smirked. "I can't offer you that, but how does rabbit stew sound? I caught one earlier this morning while searching for you."

"Yes, and I'll help." Anything to get my mind off how everything seemed to get worse the longer I stayed in the Den.

When Dagen and Oryn appeared in the kitchen, Nero laughed and strode over to his friend. Both thumped fists and gave each other a man hug, pounding once on each other's backs.

"Dagen, never been happier to see you," Nero began. "Even more than the time that fox-shifter gang kidnapped you."

Oryn burst out laughing and caught Dagen in a headlock,

rubbing his head. "You made up that shit so you could have a raunchy night with that redheaded fox, didn't ya?"

Okay, so maybe Dagen had a niceness in him if the men were roughhousing and joking with him. I returned to chopping up wild spinach and mushrooms on a plate on the table, listening to the chuckles and jokes about some sexy fox-shifter woman. What was so great about her, anyway? She must have been amazing if Dagen had followed her, and I glanced at the long strands of hair over my shoulders, knotted and messed up. Heavens, I must have resembled a porcupine.

"I didn't follow her, Scarlet," Dagen responded. "She kidnapped me."

With a quick glance up, all three shifters stared my way.

"It's none of my business, anyway," I said.

"What are you talking about?" Oryn asked, closing the distance between us, placing a hand on my back. He kissed the top of my head.

Dagen growled, glaring at us. "Can't you see she has a spell on you?"

I gripped my blade and backed away.

But Oryn plucked the weapon from my grip and placed it on the table, before cupping the side of my face. "Remember, you are always safe when I'm near. Never be afraid."

He straightened his posture and faced Dagen, who stormed closer, his fists curled.

"Back down," Oryn growled as he pushed me behind him.

"Please don't fight over me," I said, but my words fell beneath their growls.

"She's ours," Nero said. "Oryn's and my wolves have mated with her. And we love you like a brother, but we won't let you harm her."

Dagen paced to the fireplace and back, shadows crowding beneath his eyes. "What the hell? Has the world gone insane while I lay knocked out? She's using magic and hypnotized you. I mean, fuck, she did the same to me when I woke up, and now I can hear snippets of her thoughts."

I leaned out from behind Oryn. "Technically, I *saved* you, remember."

"What do you mean, you can read her mind?" Nero stepped in between the two shifters facing off.

Dagen smacked a palm against his own head. "Don't know, but I can't get her out of my head. Like right now, she's admiring the dimples above your ass, Oryn."

Fire scorched my insides, and I hugged myself. "Shut up. If you're in my head, don't blurt out everything to the entire world. Crap. Have you ever heard of privacy?"

His nose wrinkled, while Oryn offered me a sexy wink.

"All right," Nero started. "Let's all sit down and take this from the top. I'm confused."

We all sat around the table. Me wrapped in a blanket, and three naked men. Nero and Oryn flanked my sides, while Dagen remained across from me, eying me with a strange look of suspicion and curiosity. There was no time like the present, so I jumped right in, explaining how I'd brought back Dagen and how unappreciative he'd been, which gained me a glare from him. Even how he'd read my mind. I left out the part about him calling me "vile," as it made me cringe just remembering his hatred, and I wanted to believe it was a spur-of-the-moment thing. Yet it lingered in my head... What made him hate humans so much?

He huffed and drew my attention, staring at me as if he readied to retaliate. Right, he had a direct line into my mind. *Son of a goat. Told you before, stop listening. Can't you try blocking me?*

"Trust me," he replied. "I would if I could."

I shifted in my seat, and Oryn reached an arm across my

back, drawing me closer to his side. His comfort kept me grounded when I wanted to throw a chair at Dagen.

"That means you two are connected," Oryn said.

On my other side, Nero casually took my hand in his. "I've never read about anyone hearing someone else's thoughts."

"Neither have I," I piped in, wondering if something had happened when I'd woken him up, by driving so much of my energy into him that it had linked us.

"So, we going to bunk out here while you all make googly eyes at each other?" Dagen asked. "Oryn, your pack is still out there attacking each other, dying."

"You think I don't know that? I've been out there, facing them, while you've been lying around."

The tension in the room smothered me. "There's got to be something that triggered the change. Oryn,"—I turned to him—"you were stuck in your wolf form, just like your pack, and it's only affecting those in your territory, right?"

He nodded. "Mainly those who hunt near the Terra border, and it all happened on one day last week when we all changed."

"Then it has to be something…" I lost my train of thought because I'd bet my life the pack's problems were connected to the priestess. Her replanting wolfsbane a week ago was also when Nero had said everyone had started acting strange in the Den.

"Your priestess is claiming our land?" Dagen slammed a fist onto the table, and I flinched.

"I saw her a couple of days ago. That's why she's after me." With a fast rundown of my encounter, I gnawed on my lower lip. I should have noticed earlier, and I would have, if I hadn't been drowning in lust, running for my life, or trying to make sense of what was going on with me.

"Okay, so let's rethink this," I said. "Wolfsbane kills

wolves. Look how it knocked out Dagen with a smidgen of spray. But your wolves, Oryn, have turned feral. If wolfsbane was used, it would have killed your pack. So it's not that." Unless the priestess had used magic?

Oryn said, "So it's something else. A poison. Maybe something in the air."

"Or the water," Dagen added.

"There's a river that runs through this land," Nero contributed, "and it passes along the Terra border."

"We start there then." I'd test the water to determine if poison was the culprit. Back when I'd fallen into the river from the cliff, I'd swallowed a mouthful. An electric shock had claimed me and almost caused me to drown. I'd suspected it was just me, but what if it wasn't?

So, was Dagen right about the water?

When he cleared his throat, I looked over, and he offered me a smug expression.

Whatever. You may not be right.

He snorted a laugh.

I shot to my feet. "Let's do this. I need a bucket of water from the river and vinegar. Also, crystalweed. I saw it growing in the forest. It's a vine that climbs trees and has tiny flowers with petals that are almost translucent. I need those. We'll do some experimenting."

Nero and Oryn nodded and, without a word, headed outside.

"So, you think this'll work?" Dagen asked, his voice hopeful. I wanted more than anything to say "definitely."

I shrugged and faced him. "It should tell us if the water's been poisoned." My head whirled. But wolves might have encountered other objects or creatures, or eaten affected grass, as I'd been told animals do that to cleanse their stomachs. We were just scratching the surface. What if we didn't find a solution? Would Oryn's pack die? And would I ever get home?

"Don't worry," Dagen said, his voice anything but calming. "As soon as you help Oryn, I'll escort you to the border personally so you can leave."

I glared his way, not expecting him to sympathize or understand how I felt toward Nero and Oryn.

"And I won't." He marched into the corridor, leaving me alone with feelings I couldn't trust, and a trepidation that somehow things were about to get worse.

CHAPTER 14

I tossed another log onto the kitchen fire, embers sparking, and I backed away until it settled, thankful I still wore my blanket. With a kitchen towel in my hand, I lifted the lid off the cauldron and stirred the rabbit stew with a wooden stick. The warming aroma of rosemary and onions left my mouth watering. The red wine didn't give off a strong smell, but it would add strong flavor. The potatoes were cooking in the simmering sauce.

Back home, I would make stews with mushrooms at least once a week, and Santos would eat two bowls. What was he doing now? Worrying about me? Or had the priestess taken him? I gripped the utensil and guilt chewed on my insides. Too long I'd lingered here. I had to return home.

The wind buffeted against the front door, shaking it on its hinges.

I glanced up, expecting the men to return. But they hadn't, and they'd been gone for ages. Add to that, Dagen remained somewhere in the house. Fine by me that he kept his distance. Why would I want to hang with a human hater?

Taking a deep breath, I pushed those emotions aside and

checked on the bread I'd prepared in the smaller pot after discovering a box of goodies under the table—flour, root veggies, seasoning, and two bottles of wine. The wolves tried different foods, which surprised me, including a packet of hard-boiled candies I'd found. Did Oryn have a sweet tooth? That made me think about my special chocolate cake with dates I could have baked for him if he'd had the ingredients.

Wait! What was I doing? Settling down and cooking as if this were my home? Sure, Nero insisted his wolf picked me as his mate, but we lived in different realms... worlds apart. I had a business in Terra, and shifters weren't allowed there.

The outside door blew open, and I jerked around, grasping the stirring spoon.

A flurry of wind gushed into the kitchen, ripping the dried herbs off the hooks on the wall and tossing them across the table.

Oryn stepped inside, nude and carrying a small skinned boar over his shoulder. He smirked and glanced at his bounty and back at me. "We're feasting tonight." He dropped the gutted and cleaned carcass on the table.

"But I just prepared rabbit stew."

Oryn made his way to the cauldron and peeked inside. "That's a snack for me, let alone all of us."

Nero marched into the room without a stitch on, not that I expected it since they were always naked. Yet it still caught me off guard. Nudity might be something Bee was more comfortable with, since she talked about men all the time, but it still made me giddy.

He kicked the door shut behind him. He was carrying a bucket of water, his other arm cradling a tree's worth of crystalweed vines bundled into a huge ball.

"You brought the entire plant? Just a few petals would have sufficed, but thanks," I said.

He dropped them on the table near the dead boar and

brushed at dried leaves stuck in his hair. "There's a storm coming, and I wanted to make sure you wouldn't send me back into the woods for more."

I approached him and plucked out a twig he'd missed. His hands casually reached for my hips and pulled me against him. "The stew smells divine. We'll snack on it now, and I'll set up the pig on a spit on the fire so we can enjoy it later."

On my tiptoes, I stretched up to his lips, brushing mine against his. The coldness outside had left his skin cool, a refreshing change to the heat in the kitchen. I mewled, loving how my body responded to him.

"You're adorable, little lamb. One day, I want to show you the Den, the splendors in our world."

"I'd love that."

When another set of hands found my shoulders from behind, I looked up to Oryn, who smiled his devilish grin. "Missed you." He bent forward and kissed me with the savagery that was him, leaving me flustered with arousal. My nipples hardened beneath the blanket I wore.

I came up for air and chased my breath, unable to stop my roaring pulse. Being sandwiched between two hunks didn't happen often.

Nero glanced down at the small boar and sighed. "Be back in a sec. Need to grab a long piece of wood for the spit. Oryn, keep her warm for me."

"Don't be long," I replied, cold from his leaving my side.

Oryn held me tight, my back against his chest, both of us watching Nero rush outside. The moment the door shut, Oryn guided the hair off my neck and his lips found the soft spot behind my ear.

"I meant what I said before. I couldn't stop thinking about you, how I'd take you into my arms when I returned, and how perfect we feel together."

When his hand skipped down my stomach and to my

thighs, I chewed on my cheek.

"I dream of fucking you." His voice darkened with a sexy growl. "You're on my mind nonstop."

Softening against him, I wrapped my hands behind his neck. "You get me horny with just your words."

His fingers grazed the curls between my legs, and my adrenaline hitched into high gear. The wind outside howled, the house rattling, and I wouldn't be anywhere else but under Oryn's spell.

"Sharlot... how much do you want me?" He pried open my lower lips, and a finger glided along my silkiness.

I trembled, unable to hold myself up without his support.

"I'll suck that pussy of yours dry."

"Heavens," was all I managed, when a snarl came from behind us.

We both looked around to find Dagen, fury warping his features.

"Of all the fucking bullshit in hell, must you do that while you're in my head?" he bellowed.

"Nothing's keeping me away from her," Oryn replied with his sexy baritone.

"At least hold off until we find a solution to get us unconnected," Dagen snapped, and his words hurt me.

I pulled free from Oryn and readjusted my blanket that had come loose while he smelled his fingers before sticking them into his mouth.

He might as well have licked me all over, because arousal rocked through me.

"Enough!" Dagen demanded. "I don't need her getting horny in my mind."

"Turning you on too much?" Oryn joked.

"You know about my past, so I won't deign to respond to that. Cut it out." He stormed back into the darkness of the house like a damn sourpuss.

Well, he'd sure killed the mood. "Why does he hate me?"

Oryn grasped my shoulders and licked my neck, leaving me quivering with need.

"It's complicated," he said.

The outside door creaked open and Nero dashed inside with several sticks and his hair soaked, and I felt complete to have him back.

A crack of thunder boomed overhead.

"Let's set up this spit," Nero said, already collecting the kitchen towel to move the cauldron aside.

With Oryn joining Nero, I couldn't get Dagen out of my head, either; I needed to comprehend what someone had done to him. Make him understand not all of us were the monsters he imagined. I strode into the corridor.

"Man, stay away from me with that boner!" Nero laughed.

"Sharlot's got me insane over her," Oryn said.

I couldn't believe he still hadn't worked out how to pronounce my name correctly. But, then again, it was kind of growing on me.

"I can't stop thinking about her, about fucking her, holding her," Oryn continued. "Never felt this way before."

I halted in the dim hall and leaned against the wall, listening to the men. Curiosity locked my legs in place.

"Fuck, yeah. I'm the same. You think it's the real thing? Soulmate?"

Heaviness sunk through my stomach. They had doubts? But then again, so did I. Everything had happened so fast, but to hear their uncertainties crushed my soul.

"What if Dagen's right, and we're all connected by her ability?" Oryn asked. "Shit, I'd tear the world apart if that was the case."

"Me, too," Nero's voice deepened.

And that same sentiment washed over me, piercing my heart at losing my men. Sure, I'd thought about the whole magic thing, too, and maybe our proximity made us lustily crazy. But it was so much more than that—from admiring Nero's playfulness, to his passion for cooking, to him always comforting me. And Oryn reminded me of myself in so many ways, as if we'd come from the same world. I understood his mission to take charge, to safeguard those close to him. His love was too big, and I adored that, even if he wouldn't ever admit he cared for those close to him out loud. I tingled with anticipation at spending more time with them, discovering what they loved to eat for breakfast, teaching Oryn how to stroll without being on guard, and introducing Nero to aromatic spices my friend brought me from the Utaara desert realm.

Someone cleared his throat behind me.

Dagen lingered in the middle of the hallway, shadows marring his face. "Spying?" Without another comment, he returned to the bedroom.

What was his deal? Was he expecting me to follow him, or was he the kind who tossed out insults like wildfire bombs? Bang! You're dead. He had interacted with Nero in such a friendly fashion. Why not with me?

I squared my shoulders and followed him, storming into the room, my sights swinging left and right. In a dark corner, his eyes glowed from the candlelight. What the hell was he doing?

"Trying to meditate to shut you out of my head," he responded.

"Is it working?"

"Fuck no!"

I sighed and stepped closer before crashing on the side of the bed. "Why do you hate me?"

"Where do I start?" He growled, and while goosebumps snaked up my back, I refused to back away.

"You know you can't blame me for whatever human

harmed you in the past. That wasn't me. You understand that, right?"

He emerged from the shadows, broad-shouldered and stiff, arms dangling by his sides, and he glared from beneath hooded eyes. "Don't mock me, little girl."

Okay, progress. I'd take "little girl" over "vile" any day of the year.

"Don't kid yourself." He circled to stand behind me, and I swiveled on the bed, pulling a knee under me.

Dagen lounged in a seat, the same one I'd used when I'd cured him, cared for him, asked him to wake up. I guessed that meant zero now that he treated me as a nobody.

His attention locked on me—stoic and unblinking—as he poised his elbows on the armrests and interlaced his fingers across his stomach.

I lowered my gaze, landing on the thick hair crowning his privates. Heat burned my cheeks, yet I couldn't stop gawking.

"'Cock' is the word you're looking for?" Dagen blurted. "Or you could call it a 'love stick.'" He smirked, but his smile vanished instantly.

"Wow, you made a funny! Get out of the forest."

He arched a brow. "You're the one checking me out. Does that mean I get the same privileges?"

I twisted and shuffled across the bed to face him and swung my legs off the edge. "Is that what you do with females in your pack?"

He shrugged and fell silent.

"So," I said. "What's wrong with humans in your eyes?"

"You go right for the jugular, don't you?" His attention dipped to my neck.

Was he considering how he'd rip out my windpipe? Gorge on my blood?

"I prefer meat." His words sliced through my thoughts.

"I've heard the witches in the Tritonian realm who practice Voodoo kidnap people for blood, so maybe you're mistaking my kind for theirs."

Right, he was in my head, reading my thoughts from the accidental mind meld. "They drink it?"

"Maybe. Or bathe in it. Who the fuck knows or cares? But if they step a foot in my land, I'll make them choke on their own spines."

I swallowed the thickness in my throat and stared down at my feet and the dirt under the toenails. Geez, someone was super aggressive.

"And wouldn't you be?" he asked. "After being forced into a deep sleep by a human who then placed another spell on me. And she now lingers in my mind?"

"Well, yeah when you put it that way. But I didn't plan any of this." I raised my head to face him and noted the way he now clasped the armrests, his knuckles turning white.

Dagen jolted to his feet so fast, I flinched.

"You know what I didn't plan on?" Two long steps and he towered over me. When he leaned closer, my breath wedged in my lungs, and I recoiled, resting my elbows on the mattress.

"What?" I shouldn't have asked, but the question slipped out.

"That I wouldn't be able to stop thinking about ripping off that blanket around you, spreading your legs, and fingering you until you come all over my hand. Tasting you. Bending you over and making you scream my name. Sucking on your tits until you beg me to stop."

"Oh…" I gasped. How was I supposed to answer that? Because everything he'd described sounded divine, and already scorching fire pooled between my thighs.

"And those thoughts aren't helping." He turned away, and I seized his hand.

His skin was rough against mine. I shivered and squeezed my thighs together from the heat burning me. Parsley. Juniper. Thistle. Any thoughts to stop the raging arousal between us consuming me.

He turned to face me and pulled free. "I can't be with you."

"P-Perhaps I should try using my ability on you again. To try to lacerate our connection, but no guarantees." I swallowed hard, my gaze catching the twitch of his hardening privates. My libido quivered.

"When I'm away from you," he said, "your thoughts drum in my skull. But in your presence, fog blurs my judgment, and my wolf howls in my ears to claim you, fuck you until I can't breathe. So yes, I'd welcome anything you could do to quench the madness consuming me."

But instead of me reaching over, he bent down and grabbed my ankles, lifting them and placing my feet on the edge of the mattress. His fingers trailed up my shins to my knees.

I gasped, staring at the hunk whose expression had transformed into the devil's, his eyes flooded with sexy intentions. The grin pulling his lips apart unraveled me.

"It works if *I* touch *you*." My voice shook. Tightness coiled in my stomach, my desire for Dagen heightened and throttling me at the core.

"Do it then. But I also need something to tamper the insatiability chewing me raw. A taster."

"Uh-huh." Unable to move, I lay there as he spread open my knees, revealing my most intimate parts to the man who hated me, had called me "vile," and right then, all I yearned was to be claimed.

"Show me your tits."

I unwrapped the fabric from my chest without hesitation, without concern, without a care in the world. I wanted this more than my life. The hunger he spoke of rattled me, amped up my arousal, and my pulse morphed into a bull coursing through my veins. Charging. Controlling. Overpowering.

He reached over and gingerly ran a thumb along my slit, rubbing my length, the silkiness of my heat guiding him with ease.

I moaned, collapsing onto the bed, the tingling sensation rippling through me.

Dagen stared down at me. "Pinch your nipples for me. Let me watch you pull them."

The moment a finger entered me, I arched my back. "Heavens, yes." My hands moved of their own accord, caressing the hills of my breasts, pinching my pebbled nipples, rolling them between my fingers.

Fire devoured me, and my heart raced as he pumped in and out. But when he spread my inner lips and inserted another finger, and a third, I groaned loudly and raised my pelvis, meeting his quickening thrusts.

The pleasure hurt from him stretching me, and I demanded more.

With his other hand, he rubbed my clit with a thumb, and my world floated on clouds. My body seized with euphoria, him fingering me so fast, I trembled.

"That's it, cum for me. Coat my palm."

A sudden explosion shuddered through me. I convulsed and screamed as an orgasm owned me.

Dagen kept pumping, and I writhed across the bed as the sensation rolled through me, calming me, slowing as I gulped for breath.

"Fucking sexiest thing ever." He grasped his hardness, a drop of pre-cum capping across the top.

I reached over and held his shaft, rock wrapped in silk.

He moaned. With his hand over mine, he quickened my pace. I cradled his tight balls, caressing them, teasing them.

We moved faster, and I lost myself in the way his eyes rolled back, the tightness of his chest. Seeing a man as strong as Dagen under my fingertips filled me with hope and possibilities.

"Fuck!" At once, the bulging vein on his hardness pulsed, and he nudged my hand away as he leaned over me, creamy white excitement spurting out, coating my breasts and stomach. He grunted, his warmth flooding me.

For those few moments, we stayed there, both of us drowning in elation.

"Did my touch help?" I joked, gaining me a smirk. And for the first time since meeting Dagen, I felt a closeness to him I hadn't before. He smiled as he massaged his cum across my breasts. "I could fuck you for a week straight and still crave you." His hand dipped between my thighs and tapped my clit a few times.

Shuddering, I couldn't find my words.

"But I need to understand how and why my wolf demands you're mine."

"M-Me, too." His attentiveness was magical, taking me to places I'd never visited before—horny world, more specifically. "What if what Nero and Oryn said was true? What if we're mates?"

He broke away, and I missed him already. He took a wet bandage and wiped me clean as darkness slid behind his gaze, then he wiped himself. He tossed the wad of fabric into a bucket.

"What I said before stands. I won't be with a human ever again."

"Again? So you have been with one?" I pushed myself to a sitting position.

He huffed. "Years ago, I made a promise to myself that I would never forgive humans for what they did. And each time I look at you, I'm reminded of the past, the atrocity, the pain that twists a blade in my heart."

He retreated, and I was on my feet, naked, not caring. "Please, Dagen. This moment might have meant nothing to you, but it's it means so much to me, and you've just opened a box to an emotion and attraction I can't lock away again."

Dagen growled. "Don't make false promises." His nose wrinkled and anger blared through his deep voice. "When it comes down to it, you will always turn against wolves. It's what your kind does."

Rage shot up my spine, and the words flew from my mouth. "Stop pigeonholing me into whatever shit happened in your past. I'm not whoever hurt you. Can't you understand?"

He sighed. "I may desire you like no other, my heart may race for you, but in my mind, I can never forget the wrongs. I see humanity in you. Death and my hunger for revenge. I'm sorry if you think something is happening with us, but beyond pure animalistic urges and whatever spell you've put on me, nothing else exists."

Tightness gripped my chest. How dare he toss me aside? And once again, he'd made me feel half the person I was.

My throat thickened and tears pinpricked my eyes.

He glared down at me, his lips twisting.

I couldn't stop myself and punched him in the arm. "Fuck you! You'd be lucky to have someone like me. And now your fantasies will linger on the taste I so graciously let you have, because you'll never touch me again."

Biting down on my lower lip to stop from crying, I swiped the blanket up and marched out, holding my head high. Yet on the inside, I crumbled, died at his words. But I refused to let myself go there, not while the prick invaded my mind.

Yep, that's you!

CHAPTER 15

With the blanket wrapped around my chest, I tucked one end in under my arm and stood outside the kitchen door for a few moments.

Don't cry. Don't cry.

I wiped the tear threading down my cheek. Why did Dagen bother me so much? Why the hell did I crave him as if my life depended on it? Honestly, what I needed was to get out of the Den, because, near shifters, I turned into a sex-starved idiot. But the focus was on helping Oryn and his pack, then heading home. Distance would allow me to clear my head and decide if my emotions were real or not.

I pushed open the door and stepped inside, the savory aroma of the roasting boar welcoming me. Nero was serving rabbit stew in four bowls, while Oryn lounged at the table, tearing a chunk off the bread loaf with his bare hands. They met me with smiles and warming glances. Then why did I feel their affection for me was undeserved? And they acted as if they'd heard nothing, but I was convinced they had.

They'd been nothing but caring and adoring, and my

heart beat for them. So I shouldn't have wallowed over Dagen or daydreamed about him.

"Just in time," Nero said. "Come. You must be famished."

Oryn tapped the chair beside him and winked at me to join him.

"Smells divine." The aromatic scent engulfed me, and I slipped into the chair next to Oryn. He kissed me on the cheek.

"Dagen's wolf has claimed you, hasn't he?" he asked, softness in his voice.

"I don't want him to claim me." I slouched in my seat, and Nero joined us.

He lifted my hand and pressed my knuckles to his mouth. "You will always have Oryn and me, no matter what."

I smiled and leaned into his chest. Nero's fingers were feather-soft across my arm.

"You're both incredible. After the meal, I'll run the test on the river water."

"Perfect. We might finally understand what's going on here," Oryn said, and he offered me a piece of bread as Dagen strolled into the room.

My pulse thumped through my veins, and I kept my gaze on my stew, though I sensed his every move, the scraping of his chair, the rough tearing of the loaf, and his slurping. Yep, talk about awkwardness.

We ate, and the warmth sliding into my belly left me sated and comforted. Yet I kept smelling the boar on the spit, knowing tonight we'd be eating like royalty.

"Don't freak, but back home," I said to eliminate the silence and encourage conversation, "I only eat meat once a week."

Oryn choked on his bread and slammed his chest, clearing his throat. "Once a week! No wonder you're so tiny."

"It's just expensive, and I have free veggies and herbs in

my garden. Plus, most townsfolk eat that way. The royal families have personal hunters to capture deer for meat."

"Well, little lamb," Nero said before wiping his lips, "you need not worry anymore. We'll give you all the meat you can handle."

Oryn burst out laughing and slapped the table. "Man, are you referring to food or your sausage?"

Nero shoved Oryn in the shoulder. "She loves my bone and can't get enough."

I chuckled, heat climbing up my neck. I shouldn't have been embarrassed since I was used to Bee's sexual jokes. Though Nero had a point. I offered him a grin and licked my lips.

"She hasn't tried Dagen's yet?" Oryn blurted.

I froze, not daring to look Dagen's way, unsure how to react. Would he growl and storm out of the room? I'd given him a hand job, but he'd never entered me fully... and the fact that Oryn knew this told me they'd heard us. Or he was simply fishing for information.

Dagen smirked and reached down to grab himself. "I'm packing more meat than both of you."

"Ha." Nero threw the rest of the bread at Dagen, who caught it in his other hand. "You're dreaming."

"So it's true," I said. "Dudes compare sizes? I thought only girls talked about this stuff."

"To clarify." Oryn lowered the bowl from his mouth. "We never physically compare."

"Bullshit," Nero blurted out. "Remember that time we encountered that tiger shifter and he couldn't stop gawking at your junk? He was comparing."

"What? He was jealous. Simple as that. Everyone knows tigers don't pack great ammunition. If you want a real man, it's wolves all the way." Oryn leaned against me and kissed my cheek. "Isn't that right?"

"I can't speak for tigers, as I've never seen one. But in relation to normal men, let's say you three are the abnormality in the best way, or every single female needs to move to the Den and get herself a hunter." I waggled my eyebrows, and Nero chuckled.

I chanced a glance over at Dagen, and he watched me while biting into the bread. Was he remembering I'd said something similar to him when he was unconscious? Remembering how I'd helped him? Remembering I was the good person here, not someone who would hurt him intentionally?

Outside, the wind howled, and the door rattled. The drumming of rain struck the roof, yet in the kitchen, heat cocooned me. I loved storms when I was at home in front of the fire. I'd read a book under a blanket on the couch.

With our bowls empty, Nero cleared the table, Dagen reclined in his seat, and Oryn brought the bucket of river water to the table.

"Okay, let's do this." I crouched near the vines and plucked free half a dozen translucent petals. With Oryn bringing the vinegar, I prepped to test for toxins.

I filled a small bowl with vinegar and tossed a petal inside. No reaction. I needed to confirm the acidity wouldn't impact the flower. With a few sprinkles of the river water into the same bowl, I dropped two petals into the mixture.

Alongside me, Oryn and Nero both stared at the experiment.

"It's changing," Nero called out.

Black dots formed on both translucent petals, spreading like lava, and within seconds, they both turned a charred tone.

"Is that what I think it is?" Oryn asked.

"Yep," I replied.

Dagen stood and approached us, so I added two more petals into the bowl for him to view the results.

I retreated as all three gawked at the evidence. "It's a simple test, but accurate. Any toxins present will react to the crystalweed petals."

Oryn glanced at me, his cheeks ashen. "So the river has been poisoned?"

"I'm afraid so."

"At least we're narrowing it down."

Nero patted Oryn on the shoulder, then faced me. "So, what poison is it?"

I scratched my head as all three shifters studied me. "I don't have the herbs with me to check. To determine, I have to run dozens of tests on water samples to see what plant reacts with it. It's a process of elimination. And in the meantime, no one should drink any water from the river until we find a solution. Maybe we can find other sources and determine if they're poisoned."

Oryn was pacing to the door and back, his fists curled by his side. "I'll murder the priestess. Rip her spine out and shove it up her ass."

Fear looped around in my head that if he went off like this to the priestess, he could get himself killed.

"But I've seen no other animals go feral," Dagen added.

"Meaning, something specific was used to target wolf shifters," I said.

"Then we leave now," Oryn said, reaching for the door handle.

"We're not going anywhere in this storm." Nero moved to stand near his friend. "Let's have an early night and we can depart at first light. Hopefully, the rain will have passed by then and the wolves will be sleeping."

I joined them and placed a hand on Oryn's waist, pressing up against him, and he wrapped me in an embrace. "I'll do everything I can to find out what poison it is and heal your pack."

"That means the world to me."

Nero nodded. "We'll do this together. I'll take Scarlet to her house in Terra to run the tests."

For days, I'd been eager to return home, and now that it was happening, I hesitated. The whole idea of facing the priestess sat on my mind like a boulder. Would she be waiting at my store? Should I head into Terra alone to avoid the guards apprehending my men? Talk about asking for a death sentence! And if I got caught, I wasn't dragging them into my troubles. Maybe I'd get them to wait for me at the border between our lands.

"Me, too," Oryn added. "We'll combine forces to face any attacking wolves."

I inhaled their musk and timber scents, closing my eyes. Both men held me, and their company felt familiar and like home. Still, Dagen came to mind, a part of me yearning to have him with us. Such thoughts were silly, and he'd made it clear as day where we stood.

"So, you in, Dagen?" Nero asked. "The more the merrier."

He huffed, and I glanced over my shoulder as he collapsed in a chair, his expression dark.

I'd love to have you with us.

His head jerked up and he met my gaze. For those few moments, I swore he'd apologize for his earlier words, stroll over, and take me into his arms. Instead, he climbed to his feet and turned toward the hall, vanishing.

"Give him time," Oryn said.

An explosive peal of thunder detonated outside, and Oryn tightened his hold.

Nero headed to check the roast. "Almost done."

Despite the delicious aroma, I'd lost my appetite.

Except the ache in my gut went beyond dealing with the

priestess but was also about admitting to myself I'd have to choose how I dealt with the shifters. Did I move in with them, or did they relocate with me? Heavens, this was moving too fast. Except the cold hard truth slapped me in the face. They had packs depending on them, and they couldn't go.

But I couldn't leave my shop... everything I held dear about Grandma was there. But departing from the men... I couldn't take another breath. I might as well chop off a leg. No solution came to mind, only heartache.

I cringed at knowing Dagen tapped into my insecurities, my problems, my yearnings. Well, considering I had no control over him or my thoughts, I had to accept he'd be privy to every crazy notion that went through my head.

Joining Nero near the roast, I sprinkled salt across the meat. "Delicious."

"Once we help Oryn, I'll introduce you to my pack. They will love you, spoil you with anything you desire."

"You think?" I chewed on a hangnail. "They won't hate me for being human?"

He shook his head. "Nope. Not when they see how amazing you are, how much you mean to me. Hunters have taken humans as mates in the past. It's not illegal in the Den."

I bounced on my toes. "I can't wait." And I meant every word. The dread of our mission going wrong twirled in my mind, but I couldn't deny what my heart pined for.

* * *

"What's poking my butt?" I squirmed and shifted onto my back on the bed of furs as I lay between my two shifters.

"Little lamb, that's all me." Nero laughed and pressed himself up along my hip, his hardness nestled against me.

Oryn was on his side, my head resting on his outstretched

arm. "We'll have no problems keeping warm tonight. So you can lose the other blanket." He scanned the fabric still wrapped around me.

Hell, I'd considered it, but then what? We'd get it on in a threesome? "What if you can't control yourselves?"

Nero nuzzled up against my ear, his hand across my stomach. "Who said we needed to behave?"

"You really know how to make a girl blush. Geez, I've never been with men like either of you before. No one has ever touched me the way you have or brought me to orgasm so hard. But being with two men at once... That's new."

"No, no," Oryn said. "Not at the same time. But I have no issues with watching." He leaned in, his lips grazing mine. I softened beneath him, hungry to have him.

When I came up for air, Nero gently turned my chin to face him, his mouth kissing me with a passion coaxing a mewl. Oryn ran a finger across my collarbone and dipped toward my cleavage. He peeled back the fabric of my blanket dress, unwrapping me, and caressed my breasts.

I shivered with temptation, staring at the two men devouring me with their devilish stares. "You two will be the death of me with your kisses."

Nero laughed and rolled me onto my side. He nudged my leg over his and he lifted me to straddle him. "Little lamb, time to show us how those gorgeous tits of yours bounce. And I promise to make it worth your while."

CHAPTER 16

*M*y eyes fluttered open to darkness. A faint light called my attention to the corridor, where an orange glow from the fireplace flickered on the wall. Oryn's and Nero's heavy breaths told me they still slept alongside me, legs entwined across my body. Every inch of me tingled from last night's marathon and left me feeling tender down there. Who would have thought being watched would have turned me on so much? Now, I lay next to them, adoring their warmth and their constant admiration, yet the earlier worry crept forward. The one that reminded me we would head back home today. My stomach hurt. I wasn't ready to face the priestess, or the decisions coming my way. Most days, I had enough trouble deciding what to wear.

With the urgency to pee pressing on my bladder, I wriggled out of the men's hold, took my small blanket, and tiptoed around them before hurrying down the hall, where I spotted light pouring from around the ajar kitchen door. Was Dagen awake? After a visit to the bathroom, curiosity got the better of me and I poked my head inside.

"Morning," Dagen said, his voice gravelly, clear he'd just

woken up, too. He sat in a chair, leaning over folded arms on the table.

"May I join you?" I didn't wait and wandered in, pushing the door closed to avoid waking the men. "How can you tell what time it is in here with no windows?"

He pushed himself back into his seat and stretched, his spine cracking. "Hunters can sense the rising and falling moon, so it lets me know when the sun's about to rise. It ripples across my skin, as if I'd jumped into a freezing river, like now." He stuck out his forearm.

I stepped closer and studied the way the hairs on his skin shifted upward. "Impressive internal wake-up alarm."

"Yep."

I glanced around the kitchen, unsure if I could head back to sleep if it was morning, and my stomach was doing somersaults. Half the loaf I'd baked yesterday remained on the table. "Want egg toast?"

"No idea what that is, but sure. I may be a hunter, but my favorite ingredient of all time is eggs."

I took the bread and set it in front of him, then fetched him a knife. "Cut these to the width of one finger."

"The bread's hard. You sure this is edible?"

"You bet. Means the slices will soak up more of the yummy goodness and helps ensure the result is not soggy." I busied myself with placing a pan over the fire and used a slice of fat from the leftover piggy for oil. Yesterday, I'd found a container of eggs in the boxes of supplies under the table, so I pulled them out. With four of them beaten in a bowl, I dipped two pieces of the loaf he'd cut into the mixture and placed them into the frying pan. At once, the delicious aroma hit and my mouth watered.

Taking a seat next to him, I coated more bread. "Eggs are my go-to meal, too, when I can't be bothered to cook. I could eat them for every meal. But where do you men get eggs from here?"

"Back in my territory, my pack runs a farm of animals, including chickens, and a garden to supply food to everyone year-round."

"Really? I thought you would chase anything you needed." I got up and flipped the slices, oil splattering, and I backed away.

"We hunt any day we want, but we like variety. We also hold a monthly pack run under the full moon to bond as a pack, so we're not complete savages."

"That sounds like it would be kind of fun, if I were a wolf. During full moons, I always cleanse my herbs. They say that such nights can clear away impurities." With a plate in hand, I scooped up the slices and placed them in front of Dagen. "Enjoy."

With the next two in the pan, I took the salt to the table to find the food gone and Dagen licking his lips. "What did you call this again? It's good."

"Egg toast. It's even better with salt." I set the salt bag down.

"Gotcha. So tell me. Do you think once we're apart, our connection with each other will break?"

"Maybe. Or you could be stuck with my funny thoughts in your head for life. Who knows? The universe has a strange sense of humor."

"Funny thoughts? Let me know when you have any of those so I can laugh." He smirked. "So far, it's all been you getting horny, worried about losing Nero and Oryn, and facing the priestess. Kind of repetitive if you ask me." He leaned back in his seat, his brow cocked.

"There's more. I've thought about you lots, too."

He shifted in his seat. "Why does it bother you so much whether or not I like you?"

The sizzle of the oil drew my attention, and I hurried to turn the egg toast. "I don't think it's fair to judge me with the same stick you do for all humans. Everyone's different."

"True."

Back at the table, I sat down. "What? You're agreeing with me! Wow." It was progress.

He didn't respond but studied me as if I were a strange creature he'd never seen before.

"My grandma used to say no matter someone's race, we are unique and have both good and bad inside us."

"She sounds wise."

"I miss her so much." On my feet, I collected the egg toast, added a new batch, and returned to my chair. "Some days I wake up and swear she's in the house. I once even called her name as if she were still alive. How crazy is that?"

"Not at all. I mourn my brother to this day. Some days, I feel like he's near me, and I talk out loud to him."

"I do the same." I reached over and touched his hand, knowing too well the agony of losing someone close to you. "Sorry to hear about your brother. Was he younger than you?"

Dagen nodded. "Years ago, I had stupidly fallen for a human girl, Marian, when she had crossed over into my territory. Like a fool, I made plans to propose to her like your kind does. When she hadn't come back for over a week, my brother secretly went to find out why. But he never returned home. So I took off to find them, only to discover my brother hung by the throat, dead, and paraded in the middle of the town. Marian was there, calling for the deaths of all wolves, insisting we'd kidnapped and raped her."

He dropped his head.

"Shit! Why would she do that?" I didn't recognize the name, or I might have asked Bee to cast a curse on her.

He lifted his gaze, and his eyes glistened. "A week later, I abducted her for real, to discover the truth. Turned out I was just a fun time, and when her parents spotted her talking to my brother, who was naked, she panicked and told them a lie. She apologized for my brother, but how the fuck could she stand there and just say *sorry* for getting someone killed? That day I lost a part of myself. I could handle breaking apart when she wasn't my true mate, but I'd been a fucking idiot. To bury my kin because of my mistake tore me apart."

My insides curdled. *Hell!* "Oh, gods, that's horrific." I tightened my hold on his hand when a burned smell hit me, and I jumped up and flipped over the slices in the pan.

"Losing anyone is horrific enough, but that... I'm so sorry." I approached Dagen, not waiting for his response, and took him into an embrace as he remained in his seat.

His hands seized my waist, and his warmth leeched onto me. My thoughts flew to my parents, the day wolves had mauled them to death.

I held on to Dagen. That same rawness spread through me now, convincing me I'd forgotten how to breathe. I hadn't wanted to live, and for years I'd hated wolves, wanting everyone to die gruesomely.

Dagen shifted and looked up at me, his arms still on my hips. "I didn't know you lost your parents to wolves. Which pack was responsible?" His voice darkened, and he rose to his feet, towering over me. With a swivel, he sat me in his chair and he crossed the room to the skillet, checking on the toast.

I scanned the pile of toast. I picked up a piece, sprinkled it with salt, and jammed it into my mouth and taking a big bite, needing something other than the ache in my heart to concentrate on.

Swallowing the last mouthful, I replied, "No idea, but does it matter? The damage is done."

Dagen crouched in front of me, taking my hands in his, a

wrinkle capturing the bridge of his nose. "How did you stop hating wolves after what they took from you?"

"My grandma helped." I smiled, though Dagen's face blurred beyond tears. "She always reminded me that nothing is ever clear-cut. There are reasons things happen, secrets I perhaps wasn't aware of. 'Wolves don't just attack,' she used to say, but, whatever the reason, I couldn't hold an entire race accountable for what a few had done."

He smiled, and softness captured his expression. "Your grandma could have taught me a few things, I'm sure."

"She would have liked you. She always loved a challenge." I laughed, and Dagen joined in, the sound comforting, as if he'd finally allowed himself to breathe.

On his feet, he cooked the next batch. For the first time, a sense of calmness seemed to engulf him. Gone was his constant frown. I hated telling people about my parents, but I couldn't keep him out of my mind.

"I'm glad I found out," he said. "Makes me feel less alone."

"Misery loves company." I dipped the last slices into the egg mixture, ready for the pan.

Dagen grabbed another slice to eat as Oryn entered the room.

"What smells so divine?" His gaze landed on the stack, and he gravitated toward them. He claimed two pieces and gobbled them in a few bites. "Why didn't you make these for us before?" He stared at Dagen for a response.

"Wasn't me! Scarlet made breakfast."

"Girl, just when I thought you were perfect, you've blown me away." Oryn went for his third.

Nero staggered into the kitchen, half his hair sticking into the air. He headed for the plate and snatched two slices. "Okay, were you all going to eat these without telling me?"

Reclined in my seat, I gnawed on my lower lip as I checked out the three men standing there naked, gorging on food, and I'd never felt more at home in their company. We belonged together, and despite not understanding how such strong emotions clung to my heart, not a smidgen of doubt remained.

Dagen wiped his lips and announced, "I'm coming with you to Terra."

"About time you came around." Oryn fist-bumped him, and Nero hugged him with a single slap to the back, while jamming more food into his mouth.

"But I'm serious, Sharlot." Oryn said. "I need you to make more of this once we get to your place."

I nodded, yet my head buzzed with the words *your place*. "Once you take me to the border, I'll go on my own to test the river water in my store. The priestess and her guards would kill you on the spot."

"No," Dagen insisted. "I'm not letting you out of my sight if there's a chance you're in danger. We will be in our human forms in Terra, so no one will suspect us."

"Agreed," the other two said in unison.

I huffed. "Hope you're right, because I can't risk you getting caught in Terra."

"We're the masters of stalking. We've got this," Oryn added.

Nero darted out of the room while Dagen collected an empty jar from the kitchen and poured river water from the bucket into it. Right, he was on top of the plan already. I was on my feet as Nero reappeared, holding on to my bag with one hand and my red cape in the other.

"These are yours, little lamb."

I snatched my belongings, and the crimson cape slid across my hand, torn in half. The last time I'd seen it felt like a lifetime ago, a time when I'd sworn my world was under my control. But ever since entering the Den, my world had turned upside down. And now I was about to return home with three wolf shifters. My breaths sped, and I pressed the cape to my chest.

Dagen was there, massaging my back. "You'll be all right. Focus on the mission. Find a solution for the toxic river. Everything else comes later. Okay?"

"Yes, thank you." I stuffed the jar of water into my backpack and was about to jam the cape in there when I had a better idea.

Setting my bag on the chair, I unwrapped my blanket and let it fall down to my feet.

The shuffling in the kitchen died, and I glanced up to find three sets of eyes fixed on me, starved hunger behind them. I laughed. "Geez, doesn't take much to get your attention."

I placed a strip of red material around my chest and tied it up between my breasts to ensure it stayed put. The other half of the cape I fashioned into a skirt that fell halfway down my thighs. My clothes were probably torn to shreds in the woods from when Oryn had tossed them away.

"Okay, what do you think?" I asked and twirled on the spot.

"Think I need you to bend over, then I can give you my opinion," Nero teased, his hand rubbing the tip of his cock.

I rolled my eyes. Another reason they couldn't go into Terra, being naked all the time. "How about we do that later."

"Just remember, little lamb, I'll hold you to that promise. And you'll wear that little skirt, right?"

I blew him a kiss. "You bet."

"Now I'm jealous," Oryn said. "I want in on this. Bet Dagen does, too."

Each of them looked over at Dagen, who wore a mischievous smirk, and my cheeks heated, remembering our little time together in the bedroom, and how I'd love to continue that. But just because he'd shared his past with me didn't mean he wanted anything else.

"Let's do this." Nero opened the outside door and a cool breeze swished inside, coiling around my legs. Oryn tracked after him, and Dagen came up from behind me. His presence burned into me, boiling my blood from my head to my toes and everywhere in between.

His fingers found my waist, and his mouth was on my ear.

I trembled.

"Such a shame you can't read my mind." He strolled into the outdoors, leaving me shaken and alone in the house.

Heavens! I craved Dagen as much as I did the other two, so how was I supposed to handle three of them while terrified of what would happen once we crossed into Terra?

CHAPTER 17

"*I*s that my boot?" I pointed to a boot sitting on its side right near the river's bank. Please let it be. Already rocks and twigs had stabbed at my feet.

Oryn released a knowing growl and leaped forward in his wolf form, his black fur fluttering in the breeze. He launched out of the forest and targeted the river bank.

Dagen sniffed the air, his gray head pivoting right, then took off.

Nero edged in front of me, his white pelt soft against my legs, and he grumbled, pointing his chin toward a dead log where I could sit down.

"You read my mind." I hobbled over and flopped onto the wooden seat. Crossing my legs, I rubbed my sole and plucked out a pebble pressed into my heel.

Nero sat next to me, his tongue hanging out as he studied our surroundings. I scratched his head, which twitched beneath my touch.

"Doubt you ever get cold in winter with all that white fur. It's beautiful."

He twisted to face me, making a protesting sound.

"Oh, right! You have a handsome, manly coat." I smirked to myself.

With the crunch of twigs, he jumped to his feet, and I spotted Oryn and Dagen trotting closer, each with a boot in his mouth. They dropped them in front of me, and I clapped.

"I can't tell you how amazing you men are, otherwise, one of you would have to carry me."

Oryn hopped closer, his head high, as if showing me his back was strong and ready.

I reached over and fluffed his fur. "You're the sweetest."

Nero wriggled himself between Oryn and me, making a yelping sound, offering himself.

"Ha, you two are funny." My gaze lifted to Dagen, who sat there, studying me, his ears pointy. So I pulled on my boots, my toes exposed from the rip across the leather on one foot. Teeth marks dotted the next one. But the soles were intact, and, standing up, I swore I floated on air.

"I can now run a marathon." Up close to Dagen, I leaned over and hugged him, his warmth leeching onto me. "Thank you." Then I stood, and we started off again.

Oryn led the march, as this was his territory and he had earlier insisted we take a longer path to avoid cliffs and wolves. Nero walked at my side, and Dagen behind, meaning no one could sneak up on us.

We hurried past dozens of pines, trampling over bushes. Foliage and broken branches littered the forest floor. We moved fast, the morning sun piercing the canopy overhead, warming my shoulders.

The deeper and farther we traveled, the more my gut clenched. What would I find back home? The priestess parked outside my shop, ready to arrest me? Or apprehend all of us? Would Santos be okay? What if townsfolk saw me with three naked men sneaking through the woods?

Yep, because, as if getting one star on the Customer Approval Plank wasn't bad enough, what would I get now?

Chased out of Terra with pitchforks?

My breaths sped up, and I hugged my stomach. Surely not. But then, what?

A bird screeched, and a flock of crows crossed the skies.

By some miracle, we'd had a smooth passage and now the sun had reached high noon without a single encounter with wolves. Oryn's suggested route had worked like a charm as we now crossed an open field. Yellow flowers littered the meadow, and the grasses tickled my knees. Warmth beat on my back and shoulders.

Nero and Oryn leaped farther ahead of me like race-horses, pouncing and tumbling into one another. Something tinged deep in my chest. A sensation that my life was where it should be.

Dagen strode alongside me. Now and then I scuffed his fur. He rewarded me with gorgeous big eyes, staring my way, unblinking. Mesmerizing.

Woods surrounded us once we'd reached a middle point in the open meadow, branches swayed, and the breeze picked up, bringing with it a chill.

When a howl echoed behind us, I spun around, my hands clasped to my chest.

Half a dozen wolves burst out from the forest, fanning out and charging.

My heart slammed into my ribcage so hard, I swore it would break out. "Hell no." I'd had enough of running for my life and fighting wolves to last me an eternity.

Dagen hit my thigh with his head and grunted.

Yes, move!

I whirled and darted, gripping the straps of my bag over my shoulders to stop it from bouncing about. The earlier glee twisted into trepidation. I pounded the ground, and already Oryn and Nero were charging in my direction, their fur bristled.

They whizzed past me in a zoom, targeting the wolves at my back. Dagen remained close, and I sprinted faster than I thought possible.

Snarls erupted behind me. I couldn't look, not when my skin crawled as I pictured myself mauled to death.

In the meadow, we remained open targets. More so me. I was the vulnerable human the wolves saw as food. That thought squeezed my lungs, and I sprinted faster.

My breaths raced, a cramp settling in my side. I pressed a palm over the pain and kept going. Nothing would stop me. The woods were about fifty feet away now, meaning more of a chance to find a weapon to defend myself, somewhere to hide.

Dagen fell behind, and the thundering growls were right in my ears.

I dared a look over my shoulder, and Dagen was tangled with two wolves, my other men in their own fights, but one wolf, brown as mud, circled the battles and charged right for me.

I ran with a scream pressing on my throat.

I needed a weapon fast.

I pulled my bag off, driving one leg forward, then the other. From my bag, I grabbed a wolfsbane root.

Paws pounded the ground behind me.

Heavy breaths were on my heels.

Dread iced my insides. If I could reach the forest, I'd scramble up a tree and be safe.

I jumped over a log.

A shadow flew toward me from my right. I swiveled, screaming, and threw out my hand with the wolfsbane.

The brown wolf crashed into my side, the air knocked out of my lungs, and I smacked the ground.

Scrambling backward, I drove the plant into the animal's gaping mouth.

He fell, whining. I didn't want to hurt him, but I didn't want to die.

Another wolf rushed at me, teeth bared.

My world blurred with fear.

On my knees, I swung my bag at his face, and the force threw him sideways. I climbed to my feet, giving me enough time to spot Dagen storming ahead, head-butting the wolf so hard, he flew into a tree.

More wolves emerged from the forest behind us. I couldn't wait for the others. Despite the worry piercing my heart about whether or not they'd be okay, I spun and ran.

Reality struck me like a lightning bolt. How was I ever supposed to live in the Den if the wolves saw me as nothing but a meal? Sure, they were under an influence, but all it took was a juvenile pup, or an angry wolf attack, and I'd die. I didn't heal quickly or have the ability to fight.

I burst into the woods, foliage snapping under my heavy steps. And up ahead, I spotted the huge hedge of wolfsbane marking the border between the Den and my land. *Heavens.* The best sight in the world. I thundered onward, tearing through the shrubs, and stumbled out from their tangled branches before crossing over into Terra.

Panting, I set my hands on my knees and glanced back over the hedge. Dagen paced back and forth near the barrier. Was he worried about following? I rushed over to the plants, stepping in between them once more. I pushed my arms outward and forced them over, stepping on the stems, creating a narrow gap for my men to pass behind me.

"Come on," I yelled, but Dagen wasn't moving. I shoved the wolfsbane farther apart and widened the passage, yet he kept staring into the field, waiting for Nero and Oryn. A dark army of wolves hounded after them.

Dread scratched the inside of my skull like dirty nails on stone.

I prayed the barrier scared the wolves away and didn't make them insane enough to attempt leaping over.

Already a faint tingle pricked my arms from the toxin where I'd touched the wolfsbane.

"Hurry," I yelled.

Within moments, they were here. Dagen dashed past me. Then Oryn and Nero followed.

Climbing out of the shrubs, I forced the plants back upright to cover the gap and recoiled as dark forms appeared on the other side. My flesh buzzed and my head spun.

The animals stalked back and forth, and we had to leave in case they braved a jump to their own detriment. So I turned away but stumbled on my feet. The forest doubled in my vision.

I shook myself and refused to rub my eyes as my hands and arms remained tainted with wolfsbane. I couldn't allow the herb to hurt my men, even accidentally.

An electric sensation crawled up my legs, and I found Dagen transforming, while Oryn and Nero growled at the pack across the shrubs.

In his human form, Dagen rushed over, his face drawn with worry.

I recoiled and held my hand up between us. "Don't touch me. I've got wolfsbane on me. I think it's affecting me." Though it shouldn't be affecting me this much.

"Okay, which way to your store?" His words raced.

Where were we? These woods weren't the ones I frequented, and I kept scratching my arms. "We need to go before someone sees us." I figured if I kept going straight, I'd soon stumble across something I recognized, praying it wouldn't be a guard.

Right now, I wasn't sure what would be worse, me

arriving with the wolves or with naked men. Hell, either way, I was drowning in trouble.

A root snagged on the toe of my boot, and I tripped forward, landing on hands and knees.

The whining grunt of my wolves closed in, and Dagen offered me a hand, but I pushed myself to my feet and scratched my forearms. "I won't make you sick."

Fear sat on me like someone covering my mouth and nose. I could barely get enough air into my lungs. Getting ill wasn't an option, especially with three shifters in Terra, Oryn's pack still in danger, and the priestess after me. My insides crumbled, but I smiled at the men, putting them at ease.

Except Dagen, who stared at me with a frown, but he didn't voice his concern. Sure, he'd read my thoughts but just knowing I wasn't alone in this eased the ache slightly.

We traveled through the woods, not always in a straight line, but the trees were lifesavers, as I used them to keep myself from falling on my face. Red blotches—as well as countless cuts—covered the skin on my arms. A cold chill rolled down my spine.

Breathing hurt, and I pressed my back against a trunk for a few moments, unable to stop scratching.

"Scarlet, tell me what to do," Dagen demanded. "You're pale as a ghost."

"Basil." I pointed to the green herb surrounding us. "Chew the plant and place it all over my arms."

Dagen scanned the ground but seemed to be missing the green herb. Nero and Oryn transformed, both their wolves growing in size with ease, fur vanishing, their ears shrinking. Nero stood before me, worry crammed in his gaze.

"Little lamb, I've got this." He plucked basil leaves and handed them to Dagen and Oryn. All three chewed the green leaves, their faces scrunching before they spat them into their palms.

I held my arms out. "Place them all over my arms and my hands, but don't touch my skin with yours. It should calm the itchiness."

The chewed-up basil felt warm against my flesh, and despite our situation, I couldn't help but laugh at seeing these strong alphas masticating the plant in unison. "Can someone put fresh leaves into my mouth, too?"

Nero obliged, careful not to touch me.

By the time the green paste coated my skin, the scratchy sensation had eased, and I gulped down my mouthful, hoping it aided with my spinning head.

"Let's keep going," I said to my three naked men. It was past midday, and I wanted to reach my place before nightfall.

We traveled for what seemed an eternity.

"I smell fire," Oryn said.

Raising my chin, I smelled nothing. We kept moving until the faint smell of smoke hit me. Finally, civilization. Once we got closer to homes, I'd leave the wolves in the woods while I found out where we were.

"Not sure that's a good idea," Dagen piped in.

"Neither is rocking into town with three naked men," I hissed.

A carving on a tree we were passing grabbed my attention. A circle with a triangle inside. Protective runes. My heart soared, as I'd seen them before. I found other pines with similar markings and looked around at the gurgling creek nearby, the land sloping upward.

"Oh, I know where we are." And I pushed onward. "My friend lives here."

My thighs ached with the climb, and still my vision refused to sharpen.

Soon enough, we reached the top, where we stood at the

rear of a two-story stone house. Decorative wooden slats covered the windows and the pointy roof had an iron weather vane topped with a rooster.

Just being here had me ready to tackle the world. I turned to my men. "Stay here, please, and I'll be back."

Oryn nodded, and I headed to the front of the building, pulling down my skirt, which had inched up my thighs. But when I raised my gaze, I found Bee already in the doorway. She wore pants and a long-sleeve shirt, not her usual dresses.

Her eyes widened. "Scarlet? Where the hell have you been?"

My eyes watered at seeing a familiar face. "I wasn't sure I'd even make it back home, and then I met these wolves, and I swore I'd die."

"Holy fucking toads." She gulped, and rushed closer, her gaze to behind me.

I turned to see my shifters standing there, proud of their nakedness. Nero gripped his hips with a wink, Oryn had his arms folded, and Dagen studied us with his darkened stare.

Bee shoved me into the house to where two couches faced the fire. This was where we had spent nights chatting about boys and spells. We'd devour an entire cake between us and drink endless cups of coffee. Heavens, I missed those times so much.

She slammed the door shut and swung toward me. "Who the fuck are they? Did they follow you? Are they guards? Why are they naked?" She paced to the window to peer out. "What do they want?"

"Relax, they're with me. I have so much to tell you." I stumbled toward her, and she seized my arm, her nose scrunching as she stared at the green stuff.

"What happened to you? What's this green stuff and what are you wearing? Girl, your hair is atrocious."

"Is your dad home?" I took off my backpack and dropped it near the couch.

She shook her head. "He's at the markets. I was about to go and continue searching for you, as I've been doing for days."

I swallowed the rock in my throat and stalked to the door, opening it to the men and waving them forward. I turned to Bee. "They won't hurt you."

They strutted their stuff indoors, each one spreading out to inspect a different part of the room. Nero made a beeline for the sofa and flopped, putting his feet up, while Oryn inspected the bowl of fruit on the table in the corner and helped himself to an apple. Dagen remained near the door, unmoving, like a warrior.

It's okay, Dagen. You're safe, I promise.

Bee backed toward the window, the lace curtain fluttering around her. "Scarlet, what the hell is going on here? Have you finally snapped and are here to have an orgy?" She smirked. "'Cause I might be all in on that."

"Sounds intriguing," Nero added.

"What?" I walked to Bee's side but tripped over my slow feet. Crashing into the side of the sofa, I caught myself before landing on the floorboards.

"Whoa! Okay," Bee began. "Someone tell me who you all are or I'm pulling out my whacking stick."

I couldn't form words as I broke into a coughing fit.

"She's got wolfsbane poisoning," Nero barked, "and needs a shower to cleanse off the toxins."

Footfalls boomed, but I remained on my knees, hunched. The world tilted.

"Come." Bee was at my side and seized an elbow, drawing me outside and to the rear of the house. "I have a tub there. Dad uses it sometimes to wash himself when he works in the garden." She turned to the men. "Go into the bathroom inside and bring me several towels. Quick."

Without hesitation, they hurried indoors. They'd probably return with the entire linen closet.

Bee led me to a wooden tub near the house. "Sorry, Scarlet," she said. "We've got to do this with cold water. I'm worried you have little time if you're already passing out. Now strip and get in."

I stepped into the tub and removed my flimsy outfit made from Grandma's cape. "So much has happened," I said.

"You owe me an explanation." She pumped water into a bucket. "Why you're with three naked hunks. Why you're covered in bruises and cuts. And where did you vanish to this week?"

She brought over the pail and plonked it on the ground. With her palm hovering over the surface, she murmured a few words I couldn't decipher.

"What are you doing?" I asked.

"Just helping you heal quicker." She dashed into the back door and appeared seconds later with two sponges. She pushed one into my hand.

"Now wash and explain."

I dunked my sponge into the water and spread the liquid down my arms as a faint tingle buzzed up my flesh. Bee scrubbed my back. I flinched from the iciness, but the sun overhead kept me warm. Thankfully, she lived out in the woods alone and no one came without tripping her detector spells. I trusted Bee with my life, so I told her a super abbreviated version, leaving out the juicy details about my sexual encounters. That would come later when I had time. I did mention the whole mate thing. But I left out the part about my complication with Dagen, as I still hadn't worked out what was going on with us.

171

"Crap balls, Scarlet. Wolf shifters? Are you sure we're safe?" She wrung out her sponge before targeting the back of my arms. "I mean, if they kept you protected, then they must truly care for you. But all three of them? Is that what they do in their packs? Several men with one girl? Hell, they're sexy, too, and I'd take one off your hands if they ever get to be too much. Ha… If it were me, I'd have them all take me at the same time."

"Bee!" I twisted to face her. "I could never. Wouldn't it be awkward?"

"Ha. You have three cocks around you and you're still shy? Listen, one for your mouth, the other in your pussy, and then your ass. Simple."

My cheeks burned. "Heavens, have you been with three men at once?" Personally, the closest I'd gotten to that was being watched by Oryn while Nero and I had gone at it, and then I'd taken a turn with Oryn as Nero had looked on.

"I wish." She laughed when the three men rounded the corner of the house, their arms piled high with towels. Called it.

"Good, you're back," Bee said.

Nero moved closer. "Can you wash her breasts?"

"Hey." I tossed my sponge at him, but he ducked and it missed him.

Bee smirked and picked up the bucket of water. "Okay, horndogs. She's clean of wolfsbane. Do your thing and wipe her down."

Oryn and Nero approached, and I giggled. They each took an arm and wiped me dry, Nero zeroed in on my back, taking his sweet time on my ass, while Oryn caressed my breasts through the towel, his thumbs flicking over my nipples.

I tingled all over but didn't need to turn into a sex-slave around Bee. So I snatched the towel from him and finished drying myself.

Dagen chatted with Bee a few steps away, but I couldn't hear them. She laughed, and I loved her dearly, but still, a tinge of jealousy tugged in my chest. I climbed out of the tub with help from Nero and Oryn, then wrapped myself up.

All at once, Bee stiffened and marched closer. "Quick, Dad's home. Everyone get into the house and in my bedroom. Now!"

We all followed Bee into the house, and Nero was in my ear. "Is that code for what I think it is?"

I rolled my eyes and shook my head. "No. Her father *is* here, and if he sees any of you, he'll raise the alarms."

CHAPTER 18

*B*ee closed the men and me in her bedroom as she went to greet her dad and keep him occupied. Dagen stood at the window, staring down into the yard through the curtains, while Nero lounged on the double bed, creasing flowered sheets. The walls were littered with glittery dried flowers, and Oryn flipped open the wardrobe, revealing every color under the rainbow. Damn, I so needed to update my clothes soon.

Still in my towel, I figured Bee wouldn't mind me borrowing an outfit.

Oryn pulled out a long red dress with no sleeves and a low V-neck. "This would be perfect on you."

I shook my head. "I'm not really a skirt kind of girl."

Nero scrambled up, sitting on the edge of the bed. "They suit you. Plus, remember, you promised me a show in a skirt."

Oryn pressed the garment into my arms and, considering every other outfit in Bee's collection was a dress, I figured this was a losing battle. I removed my towel, and even Dagen reclined against the windowsill, his arms folded across his chest, as his gaze dipped down my body.

Enjoying the show?

He smirked and turned around to look outside.

I pulled the gown over my head and tugged it down over my body. It was a smidgen loose, but then again, Bee was a lot bustier than me. Still, the V-neck sat low enough to show off cleavage.

"Now that's sexy," Nero said, pawing at my dress, flattening it down my legs, and squeezing my ass. "And all ours."

Oryn poked around in the drawers of the chest cabinet and brought out a pair of pink panties.

"Put those away." I rushed closer and shoved them back inside.

"Yeah, why would you want her to wear any undies?" Nero protested.

I offered Nero a glare and my body heated up from how every conversation with them always returned to sex. Not that I was complaining, but right now wasn't the time or place to offer myself to them, as much as my libido clenched my core.

"Oh, now we're talking." Nero passed Oryn and plucked out a wooden shaft in the same of a penis, thick and smooth. "I'm loving the way your friend thinks."

The door opened, and my heart sank. I rammed the pleasure stick back into the drawer and knocked it shut with a hip as Bee strolled inside, carrying an armful of clothes.

She closed us in and froze as she stared at one of us and then another. "What? You all look suspicious as shit, you know."

"Well, we—"

I nudged Nero to shut up and said, "I... I went through your wardrobe and borrowed a dress. Hope you don't mind?"

"Of course, babe. You can borrow anything." She dropped the bundle of outfits on the bed.

"Anything?" Nero sagged onto the mattress, cocking an eye my way.

Ignoring him and the way he stared at the drawer with the pleasure stick, I approached Bee. "What are these?"

"As much as I love staring at the mens' junk, they need to put on something to fit in at Terra. Help yourself. They're Dad's, but he won't notice, as he hasn't worn these in years."

The men sorted through the outfits, and I followed Bee to the window. "Scarlet," she began. "While you were gone, the priestess messed up your store. She's after you."

I stood there, frozen, unable to move. "Is Santos okay?"

She nodded. "Yeah, I got him to live with us here, so he feels safe. He's at the markets now, selling tea to make coins to help repair the store."

My heart bled. "He's an incredible kid. In case I don't see him today, tell him I'm fine." How bad had my shop been damaged? And if the priestess was searching for me, what future did I have in Terra? What about everything Grandma had worked so hard to build?

"What are you going to do?" Bee squeezed my arm.

I couldn't respond to the reality of how shitty my situation had become. She took me into her arms and hugged me. "You can stay here as long as you need. A guard came searching for you a few days ago and, after he inspected the house, he apologized for the intrusion and left. So I doubt they would come back."

"Thanks." But my life had become so much more complicated after meeting these three amazing men. Except they didn't belong in my world, and maybe I didn't, either, anymore. But the Den wasn't safe.

When Nero chuckled, we turned to find the men dressed and shoving each other about playfully. No surprise Nero would wear the shiny vest with no shirt underneath and knee-length shorts. It suited him and his muscular arms.

Oryn buttoned up a black shirt and wore matching pants. But both pulled taut across his body and looked ready to bust open if he flexed. With his long, raven hair, he was the epitome of a shadow assassin, or what I'd imagine they looked like, hunting in the Darkwoods realm.

Dagen only had on pants the color of dried grass that reached halfway up his shins. They hung low off his V-shaped waist, drawing attention to his abs, and the delicious package cradled lower.

When I looked up, he arched an eyebrow at me. "What am I supposed to wear on top?"

"Told you," Nero said. "Put on the cape."

Dagen's death stare made me smirk. "I'm not going around looking like a bat."

"That's from a costume party," Bee said. "No idea how it got into the pile. Why not try the short tunic? It's loose and you look like a big boy."

He plucked out the sand-colored tunic and pulled it over his head. It matched his light hair.

"So, what now?" Bee said. "What are you four going to do? I'll go with you if you need help." She collected the rest of the clothes and tossed me my backpack, which I'd left downstairs.

"We need to visit my shop, as I need to test for the poison in the river and help the wolves. Plus, I have to see what state my store and home are in." I pictured the place demolished and only rubble left. I hugged myself from the chill crawling along my arms.

"Sounds like a plan," Oryn said. "We will keep Sharlot safe."

"Is that right, Sharlot?" Bee smirked my way, but when she pulled me aside, her tone turned serious. "I know this is

177

the wrong place, and I hate asking"—she twisted her fingers over one another—"but yesterday, Dad sold our last few chickens at the market. And—"

"Oh, crap. I owe you the wolfsbane for that job." I dug into the bag, certain I had two roots left. I gingerly lifted them by a thin thread. Once I got home, I'd be disinfecting everything in my bag. "Got them right here. Sorry I was late."

Bee collected a jewelry box from the chest of drawers, tipped the contents out, and presented the open container. I placed the plants inside.

"Damn, girl, you have the best excuse in the world," she said. "But I should be okay, I think. I'm only a few days late to go into the mountains to complete the job, and, fingers crossed, my new clients won't be pissed. I'll head there as soon as Dad heads back to the markets." She looked at me as she shut the box. "Unless you need me here?"

"No, we're all good. Do what you need to do. When you return, we can do a massive catch up." I hoped I would still be here.

* * *

LEAVES RUSTLED AROUND US, and the afternoon sun already dipped, but the four of us had marched through the woods, staying clear of the town and homes. The forest swayed around us. We followed the next bend. Then I halted and gasped as I laid eyes on my shop. My life. Everything Grandma had left me.

The small building with stone walls had the windows busted out, the wooden window panels torn off their hinges, along with the front door. The sign dangled over the doorway, ready to fall. My heart bled, and tears prickled my eyes.

Dagen was right beside me, taking my hand in his, while Nero and Oryn took the lead. But everything inside me trembled. I'd worked so goddamn hard to have it ripped away. I scanned the area. No sign of guards around. Were they watching? Surely if they were, they would have arrested us by now.

Dagen sniffed the air. "No one's here but us."

I ran forward, tears flooding my cheeks. Inside, I stepped on splinters, broken jars, herbs scattered everywhere. The counter sat on its side, as did the display cabinets in the front windows. Every item on the shelves on the back wall lay smashed, except a single teapot remained untouched.

Someone had even thrown my cash register into the wall, resulting in a massive hole. "Bastards," I choked, shaking, unable to deal with the loss. I fell to my knees, and the emotions strangled me. The life I'd put together had been torn away. All my hard work, the healing potions I'd created for sick people, destroyed.

Nero was next to me, his arms around my shoulders, his head against mine. "Little lamb, I'm so sorry." He took me into his arms and held me tight.

I sobbed against his chest, tired of always following the rules, doing the right thing, and yet I'd witnessed the priestess breaking the law, and I'd paid for it.

"This isn't fair," I whispered. "I wanted to help people, follow in my grandma's footsteps. I didn't hurt anyone."

He rubbed my back and kissed my head. "No one will ever touch you again."

"We'll help you rebuild your store," Oryn added.

I pulled free and wiped my eyes. "Then what? The priestess will come and destroy it again when she comes to imprison me for life or execute me."

The three of them surrounded me in a group hug, and my tears kept flowing.

"Sharlot, we'll fight the entire army to protect you." Oryn

brushed a tear away with his thumb. "We will aid you with anything."

My throat thickened. "But I was supposed to help you and the wolves." I broke out of their arms and scanned the mess around us, then stared at the doorway to the storage room, where I kept backup herbs. "Maybe I still can." I traipsed to the back room and found most of it still in one piece.

I grabbed an empty bowl I'd found on the floor and dumped my bag down, then took out the bottle of river water. My hands trembled as I picked up a jar of poison ivy off the shelf. Time to test the herbs to see if anything reacted to the poison.

"Are you sure we're safe here?" Oryn asked from the doorway as he glanced over his shoulder toward the trashed storefront.

My head spun. Was he right? What if the guards showed up any moment? "Okay, everyone grab as many of these herb jars as you can. We're leaving the store."

Once outside with arms full of jars, I rounded the building and marched deeper into the woods. I stared left and right, watching for any movements. But it was clear.

"Where are we going?" Nero asked.

"To my place. It's a bit of a hike into the woods." I'd always thought Grandma had been paranoid, having her house so far from the store and hidden over a hill, but now I couldn't be more grateful. I honestly suspected for years she'd put a camouflage spell on the property because, to date, not one person had ever stumbled across the house.

No one said a word, but we walked fast. I always traveled a different path between the store and my home. Grandma had taught me to not create a track between the two places should I ever need a hiding spot from the shop.

We climbed a slope and over the crest I found my home. I smiled and hurried forward to the two-story wooden house with a small porch out front. Everything looked intact, even the bird feeder in the field. I adored waking up to their songs.

At the door, I reached for the top of the doorframe and grabbed my spare key from the ledge.

"I'll go in first," Oryn insisted, and I wasn't arguing in case there was a surprise attack.

I waited, and Nero held my hand.

Halfway through the living room, Oryn turned with a grim look on his face, his nose wrinkled. "What is that funky smell?"

"What?" I hurried inside and the pungent smell hit me. *Right.* I had been making cottage cheese and had left it out too long.

"It's just cheese. Open the windows." My tiny kitchen had a long counter against one wall, a fire stove at the end and shelves filled with provisions. Near the window was the culprit, hanging from a horizontal stick balancing over a bucket. I grabbed the gooey mess in the cheesecloth and ran outside with it, holding my breath. Yep, it was bad. I threw it deeper into the woods behind my home, figuring I'd clean it later with the rest of the mess in my store. Now, I had to find a solution for the poisoned water, and how in the world I'd remain in Terra while the priestess hunted me.

CHAPTER 19

*B*ack inside my house, I locked the door behind me and turned to find three men studying the place. A strange sensation swirled in my stomach at the familiarity of being home, yet sharing it with shifters.

Nero ran a hand across the wooden walls while glancing up at the beams overhead. He strolled to the stone fireplace in the living room. Pinecones littered the mantelpiece. I'd had this thing about collecting them when I was young and couldn't bring myself to throw them away, as they reminded me of my parents.

"So, this is my little abode," I said. "It's nothing special, but perfect for me." Downstairs had the kitchen, bathroom, and a resting room, while on the second floor were the bedrooms.

"I love it," Nero said, picking up wood from the pile next to the fireplace. "Now to get this place warmed up."

Oryn glanced upstairs, gripping the timber banister, as if ready to launch himself upward. "Only two rooms up there?"

I looked up at the spare room that used to belong to my grandma, and how I used to tiptoe past her room when I'd woken up in the middle of the night. But she'd always heard me and would join me in the kitchen. Those nights we'd end up cooking a feast with leftovers and telling silly jokes. The best memories ever.

"Do I need more rooms?" I returned to the kitchen and lit the stove, ready to make a huge pot of tea.

"If it bothers you, Oryn," Nero called out, chuckling, "take the spare room. I'll be bunking with my little lamb."

Oryn shook his head and scaled the steps.

Dagen inspected the paintings of the forest on the walls.

"Those are mine," I said. "I've been practicing in my spare time."

"Love this image. Reminds me of you." He pointed to one with my grandma walking into the forest wearing her red cape. Within the shadows, I'd drawn three wolves watching her.

"I adore that piece."

Dagen offered me a knowing smile. "You have talent."

With everyone settled on the couch, the rest of the afternoon flew by. A fire roared, and I had made garlic toast and roasted vegetables, followed by honeyed oats. No complaints from the men, either. We all sat there, spoons clinking bowls and lips smacking.

"Okay, I'll be the first to say it," Nero said. "For food with no meat in it, this is fantastic."

"See." I nudged him with my shoulder. "You can still eat well without killing an animal."

"Not sure I'd go that far." Oryn stood and collected our plates before heading into the kitchen.

"So what's the plan?" Dagen swiveled at the end of the sofa to face me. "If the priestess is after you, her guards will return to your shop."

The meal in my gut churned.

"We can't stay here forever," he said.

"Agreed." Oryn strolled in. "We'll run tests on the river

water all night if that's what it takes. I can't let down my pack." His voice was strained.

I rushed after him and grabbed a bowl from the kitchen pantry along with a bottle of vinegar. "Let's do this. Whatever it takes."

All three joined me, their arms filled with the jars we'd brought from the store. I ignored the question of what would come next. Focus was the game plan. Help Oryn's pack. Worry about everything else later.

* * *

I YAWNED, my eyelids heavy as I sprinkled the last batch of dried leaves into the bowl of vinegar and tainted water. I didn't even bother to look at the label.

The men had fallen asleep. Oryn was on the sofa, Nero on a nearby chair, while Dagen slept on his back on the floor in front of the fire. The desire to crawl over and join them tugged at me. But instead, I stared into the bowl of water with floating particles. No reaction to any of the samples. Nothing at all, like all the other tests, and it killed me not having a cure for Oryn. His pack would continue to attack each other until what? They turned on the other wolves and butchered them, too? What if they entered Terra? They'd kill so many people.

An invisible vise squeezed my chest. I could barely get a breath in.

I didn't have time to sleep or pretend things would be all right, because they wouldn't be. What I needed were more samples to test. I picked up a candle and match, then marched outside into the night. I didn't want to wake any of the men. They deserved a rest, and I'd be back in no time. I knew the woods and would be fast.

A brisk chill encircled me, and I quickened my step. The shuffling of dried foliage sounded near.

"It's just the wind," I whispered and hurried down the slope, using the full moon overhead to guide me. I'd walked this path hundreds of times and knew it with my eyes closed.

By the time I reached the store, the hairs on my arms stood on end and it felt as if the night stifled me. But I'd seen how lazy the guards were, and I prayed they weren't hiding in the woods watching me. I once saw a guard let a thief pass him, insisting he was on his lunch break. I relied on their sloth-like nature.

I tiptoed across the dark shop, stepping on broken things that once meant the world to me; now they were scattered across the floor like forgotten memories.

My knee hit something, and I bit back the groan. I reached down and patted the corner of my counter on its side.

I set the candle down and lit the wick. At once, the room glowed dimly, and the place still resembled a disaster zone. Shattered cabinets, jars, and years of hard work. What would Grandma have thought if she'd seen what I'd caused?

I choked on my breath, unable to believe the mess I'd gotten myself into, and yet I still had no answer to how I'd deal with the priestess.

In my house slept three men who each held a piece of my heart. Considering their support and love, I held little doubt we weren't meant to be together. Whoever said a girl had to choose only one man, anyway.

At my feet lay half a cup with a moon phasing image I'd painted, along with a sachet of tobacco, and the box I used to collect coins for purchases. I crouched and opened the container. Empty. Of course.

More than anything else, I wished my grandma were

alive. She'd know what to do next. How to dig myself out of my troubles.

I searched for packets of herbs, and I found a handful, but then, shivering from an icy gust, I faced the hole in the wall. *Bastards.* The flickering candle from the wind painted shadows across the walls. Well, I couldn't sit here feeling sorry for myself. Time to get this done.

Focus. That had been Dagen's word.

Climbing over the mess behind the counter, my foot caught on something. I lost my balance. Pin-wheeling my arms, I yelped, but I fell and hit the floor with my knees. Pain raced up my thighs, and I winced.

With a sickening snap, the wooden floorboards gave way beneath me. I yelled, grasping for the shelf nearby. My knees hit solid ground a foot below.

"Shit!" Yep, that situation called for swearing.

I pushed myself free, but something stuck to my knee, and I peeled it away. A book. It had a dusty leather jacket and it was tattered at the edges, as if a mouse had been nibbling on it. I'd never seen this before.

Climbing out, I sat with my back to the wall and flipped through the pages, each page scribbled with handwriting. "Morning sickness" titled one page along with a list of ingredients. The next was for a headache, followed by healing broken bones.

A text of remedies! Had it belonged to Grandma?

I flicked through the pages. Dozens of them. Why hadn't she shared this with me? And here I'd thought she'd had all this knowledge memorized. I laughed as tears pooled in my eyes. She had always teased me about having a terrible memory, and yet she had been just the same.

The word *toxic* grabbed my attention.

Cure for Toxic Water.

I staggered to my feet and huddled closer to the candle,

memorizing the ingredients. Five items, and I had all of them back in my house. This could work as an antidote for Oryn's pack, as it talked about removing poison from a bucket of water. Maybe I could use it for the river?

I hugged the book to my chest, imagining myself embracing Grandma. Even from the grave, she'd helped me. "Thank you."

Something fluttered out from the book and landed on my boot. I leaned over and plucked a folded piece of paper.

It was a handwritten letter. Grandma's. The swirls on her *g* and *y* confirmed it.

DEAREST SCARLET,

MY SWEET GIRL, *if you're reading this, it means one thing. I've departed, and I knew you would discover my book. I counted on it. You had a knack for finding anything I hid from you. I can imagine you laughing at having discovered my secret... I will admit, my memory has never been great, so I kept the remedies in a journal. Now it's yours, my dear.*

But there is something else I have kept from you for too long. Please don't hate me, but this was the only way I could keep you safe. Sometimes secrets serve a purpose.

Wolves didn't kill your parents.

I lied to protect you from the same fate. The same monster who had taken their lives.

Our priestess slaughtered your mother and father.

"FUCK!" I shuddered so hard, the paper in my hands shook. The corner caught on the candlelight. It took at once, the flame extending, and I panicked, dropping the letter.

Quickly, I stomped the fire out and could barely catch my breath. I collected the paper and continued reading.

BY NOT KNOWING THIS, *then you wouldn't pry or try to get revenge. I did this for your own safety.*

You see, your father was a wolf shifter who had mated with your mom, a human, and they decided to live on the fringes of the Den and Darkwoods. But one day your parents came into Terra to collect you, as you'd spent the weekend with me. Except the guards spotted your father transforming in the woods near the border. Your mother tried to save him. But the priestess demanded both their deaths without a trial. Their bodies were then discarded over a cliff. The priestess had no idea they had a young child. So I kept you with me and told everyone wolves had murdered your parents.

That day I thought I would die from losing my baby girl. But having you with me kept me sane.

Dozens of times I contemplated telling you the truth but couldn't. You displayed no signs of carrying wolf blood and never changed during full moons, so I kept quiet.

Please forgive me for telling you this way, but it was a safeguard in case I didn't get the courage to let you know. I feared you'd leave me for keeping such a secret. But no matter what, you will always be my dearest, Scarlet.

I love you so much. No matter our distance.

Grandma.

SLIDING TO THE FLOOR, I sat there, gripping the letter, rocking back and forth. My head hurt, and the food in my gut roiled into a mess, ready to spurt out.

My legs wobbled beneath me, and I stumbled into the wall, barely able to hold myself upright.

The priestess had murdered my parents? I was part shifter?

Was this happening? Everything twisted in my mind. Dad was a wolf, but I didn't recall seeing him transform. This whole time, my parents' death had been a lie. No wonder I'd never had a burial place for them. No wonder my grandma had always changed the topic when I'd asked. No one in town had questioned it since most believed wolves were savages.

Tears flowed, and I didn't care. Why had my mom been butchered if she was human? There was no law against marrying shifters. The priestess just loathed anyone associated with them.

A burning fire seared through my chest, hatred driving my pulse into a frenzy. I got up and paced along the back wall, stepping over broken teapots and tea leaves. The priestess didn't deserve to live. Who was she to decide who lived or died? I ignored the irony of my thoughts because I didn't care. I just detested the priestess.

Grandma should have told me and let me make my own decision. I scrunched up her letter and tossed it toward the remedy book. The one she'd referred to when helping so many townsfolk with ailments.

None of that mattered. Not when I wanted to rip out the priestess' throat.

A guttural growl rolled through me, just as it had back in the forest when I'd encountered her relocating the wolfsbane, trying to take over Den territory.

Wait! Had I snarled because of my inner wolf? Was this why Nero had insisted his wolf had bonded with me, claimed me? As had Oryn's and Dagen's?

My breaths raced. Would my life have been different if I'd known the truth? I hiccupped my next inhale and blinked away the tears.

Grandma had lied, and I understood she'd had good reasons, yet her secret chipped at my soul.

It left me lost, questioning everything I'd thought I'd known about myself.

I rubbed my temples and looked out into the woods cloaked in night. Before I could find my thoughts, I stormed out of the store and rushed into the forest, needing fresh air, anything to make sense of my confusion.

Overhead, the pregnant moon hung in the heavens.

I turned toward my home, desperate to do something other than let sorrow swallow me whole.

Branches whacked into my face, snagged on my clothes, and I stopped near a dead log and slumped against it, crying hard into my hands. For losing my parents, my grandma, and my time with them.

A crunch of foliage came from behind me.

I jerked around, expecting one of the hunters.

Instead, a rope fell over my head. Heavy and thick, pressing down on my shoulders. I screamed.

Two figures approached, chortling like hyenas, wearing dark uniforms. Guards.

They tugged on the rope attached to the mesh, throwing me backward. Air gushed from my lungs.

"No. Please, no!" I shoved against the net, but it tightened, forcing my knees to my chest.

Dread squeezed my heart, and I yelled as they hauled me across the forest floor, the foliage tearing at my back.

CHAPTER 20

*S*harpness sliced down my arm. I woke with a startle, my eyes snapping open, and inhaled a lungful of urine stink. I gagged.

A guard stood in front of me, leering and gripping a bloody knife in his hand.

"What's going on?" I lurched forward, but my arms remained attached to the wall by my wrists, as did my ankles. I was shackled.

Terror crept along my spine because I'd been caught by the one person I had to avoid.

Around us was a room with stained walls and cobwebs hanging from the corners. Light streamed in from a window above my head, and ahead lay an iron door. This had to be the dungeon under the priestess' manor. And if the sun was now shining, had I been knocked out all night? The men would worry, and what if in their panic, they rushed through town shoving people around, transforming? They'd get themselves killed.

My stomach locked up. I wanted to turn back time, drag the sun down from the heavens, and never leave home.

The snorting guard with thin threads of hair arching across his head threw a backhand, the hilt of his knife catching on my jaw. My face throbbed. I cried out as I tasted copper in the back of my throat. But the bastard grinned, so I spat on his boots.

"I demand freedom." With my chin raised, I continued, "I've done nothing wrong."

He grimaced, as if I were a speck of mud on his clothes. "You're an illegal trespasser in our land."

"What? Are you insane? I've been living in Terra my entire life. Ask anyone." Trepidation sat on my stomach. Had the priestess seen me with the three men when they'd shifted in the forest? But that made no sense; the guards would have attacked us already. Meaning they'd only spotted me at the store. Unless they had followed us to Grandma's house and each of my men were now in separate cells, being tortured —or dead?

I gasped and fought my restraints. "Release me!"

He pressed the tip of his blade under my chin, and I held my breath.

"All shifters will die."

I couldn't find my words, not when Grandma's confession had revealed I carried wolf blood. But how did this donkey's ass know? I never should have tossed the letter aside in the store. What if the guards had read it after capturing me?

"You've been spying on us." His spittle sprayed my face, and I pulled away, feeling nauseous.

His weapon pierced my skin, and I held back the wince, refusing to let him see me cringe. "Not true."

"Yes, it is." His voice climbed. "So you can tell your inbred wolf friends where to attack first. What our weaknesses are."

My response flat-lined when the door behind him creaked open. He backed away and lowered his head.

The priestess waltzed into the prison cell, her azure gown dragging across the grimy floor, but she didn't care. Instead, she gripped her waist, drawing my attention to the line of tiny buttons running from her throat to her belly; more of them cascaded down her arms. It would have taken her ages to get dressed, but she probably had slaves to do the job. Dark hair cascaded over her shoulders, pushed off her face with a black band. But the wrinkles scoring her neck and the corners of her mouth reaffirmed her age of sixty. She'd been leading Terra for most of her life; surely it was time for her to retire.

"Scarlet." She approached, studying me with narrowed eyes. "What an interesting person you are."

"Not really," I responded. "I'm the most boring person in town. I don't even socialize."

She laughed, loud and all for show. "You have a sense of humor. Good. You'll need it."

I swallowed the lump in my throat, hating how her voice had darkened on those last few words. "What have I done? I deserve a fair trial to understand why I'm being held captive."

"Silly girl." She stepped closer and snatched a handful of my hair, forcing my head sideways.

I bit back the yelp that longed to be released.

"You've fooled everyone long enough."

"You're mistaken," I pleaded. "Please, whatever you think I did is wrong. I run an herbal store where I help people. I even helped you once, remember?"

She nodded but wrenched my head harder, and that time a small cry spilled from my mouth.

"You fooled me, offering your tainted remedy. I should have suspected you hid a secret, but I let myself believe you were a good person. Because I have a heart."

I almost choked on her delusion. Maybe a splinter of humanity remained in her soul, and she would show compassion if she found no proof of what she hinted at. Except she knew I'd seen her in the woods, taking over wolf territory.

She shoved my head back, and I hit the wall, then cringed. Yep, not a smidge of kindness left. She paced across the room like a caged tiger, while the guard stood in the corner close by, eying me with disgust.

"When we met in the woods a few days ago," she started, "you growled just as wolves do. Plus, the giveaway was your eyes had shifted to those of a wolf. And it got me curious. Who exactly was Scarlet?"

My eyes had shifted? My head screamed, well aware of where she was going with this. And I had to stop her. "That was me freaking out, nothing more. Everyone makes sounds." I spoke so fast, my words blended together. "Take your guard over there. He'd been grunting like a pig before you arrived. That doesn't make him suspect of anything. Except being in need of a wash."

His lips warped, and he raised his blade, pointing it at me. But the real threat was the priestess. She approached her protector, seized his blade, and returned to my side.

I pulled away as much as my restraints allowed.

"Funny thing is, that when I dug deeper, I discovered your parents were killed by wolves. Sixteen years ago." She tapped the side of the knife on my cheek. "And you know what else? I keep a record of every wolf I encounter, and where. Sixteen years ago, I found a wolf shifter on our land with his wife, insisting he was human."

I trembled, and fiery rage soared through my veins. In my mind, I kept remembering Grandma's words. Hatred surged on the back of my throat, but I held it tight or I might as well have signed my own death warrant.

"I...I doubt it's the same people. I watched my parents get torn apart by wolves near the border. I buried them with my grandma in the yard behind my shop. Dig up the ground, and you'll see." Hopefully, I'd buy myself time to escape with that lie, yet I kept thinking, if she hadn't mentioned my three shifters, they must still be safe, right?

Dagen! If you can hear me, run to the Den. Take the other two with you. Please.

I couldn't risk them coming here, getting caught and butchered.

The priestess flicked the blade toward me and sliced my cheek.

I flinched.

"No more lies. Your dad was a wolf, and that makes you one, too."

I gnawed on my lower lip, fear leeching into me at what she'd do next. "I don't know what you want from me. I've never harmed a soul."

"Yes, well, that's the problem." She dug her fingernails into my neck, breaking skin, and I tensed against her, my breaths spiking.

"You may not have attacked anyone yet. But it's only a matter of time before the beast inside you escapes. I won't risk the safety of my people."

"Your people hate you, loathe everything you do."

Her slap across my face came fast and left me dizzy. "Enough. Now show me your wolf side."

"Fuck you! I'm not a shifter. You kill innocent people all the time. The real monster here is you."

She didn't respond but swiped the blade between us, the sharp tip biting me across the stomach, fabric torn.

I cried out that time and hunched forward as much as my shackles allowed. The cut throbbed. Death flashed before my eyes. Earlier, I'd held on to the slim chance I'd survive, but I'd been a fool. An idiot. And now I'd perish like my parents. Leaving behind my three wolves, the men who'd made me realize there was so much more in life. And I yearned more than anything to enjoy my future with them, maybe even have a family.

But those stupid desires washed away as I faced the devil herself.

My throat thickened. "Please. I'm no different than you."

"You're nothing like me," she barked as she cut me across my collarbone in slow motion.

I yelled with pain, feeling as if a fireball had exploded in my chest. Every move felt like rusty nails digging deeper.

"Bring him in," the priestess spat. The guard rushed outside.

My heart froze, and I couldn't take a breath. Was it Nero? Oryn? Dagen?

Santos stumbled into the prison, his face ashen, his clothes torn and cuts snaking down his arms.

"No!" I cried. "He has nothing to do with this. He's my assistant at the store."

"When we spotted him at the markets yesterday, I figured he might tell us where you were. But this is so much better. The more people who see evidence of what you really are the better. Word will spread and everyone will start to see I'm was telling the truth about shifters infiltrating our land."

"Let him go. Please." Tears drenched my cheeks, the earlier cut stinging as if acid coated me. I wasn't sure which injury hurt worse. But I already knew the answer. My heart splintered for Santos.

The priestess smirked. "I'll release him when you reveal your wolf."

I boiled with anger, every inch of me shaking.

"Set him free, then I will give you everything you want." I stared at my assistant, giving him a look that demanded he run as far from Terra as possible when he got out of here. Of course I was lying, but with my fate sealed, I wouldn't allow Santos to suffer.

The priestess glanced over at Santos, who held himself tall, considering our situation, and I admired his strength. *Please goddess, protect Santos. Please let the priestess free him.*

But she turned with a frown, and my stomach dropped to my feet. She would never keep her word.

She shook her head and jabbed her weapon into my shoulder, the blade sinking deeper. Blood spurted across my face.

I screamed, convulsing. Shards of piercing pain shot through me, my vision blurring.

"Leave her alone," Santos bellowed. "She's not a shifter."

"Now!" she belched the word in my face and twisted the knife into my shoulder. "Let's show your little friend how wrong he is."

I shuddered, the rest of my body numb. My shouts were a racing stream, and tears soaked my face. Death. Was this what the end felt like—my soul ripped out of my chest?

"Hurry up, or Santos is next." She stabbed the knife deeper.

I jerked, my breaths panting, when a zap of energy clasped around me, sizzling over my skin. When I refocused on the priestess, the surrounding room sharpened in focus. A tiny rodent cowered in the corner where I hadn't seen anything but shadows before. I smelled the guard's stinky perspiration. And a growl rolled through my chest.

Heavy. Guttural. Threatening.

Revenge coated my thoughts. I'd never felt like this before. Was it my wolf?

The priestess gripped my chin, squeezing. "There you are." She shoved me back and waved a hand to the guard. "Bring her. I have all the evidence I need. We end this now!"

CHAPTER 21

The guard shoved his hands against my back, and I stumbled through open wooden doors of the manor and toward a manicured lawn waiting for us. Dense trees surrounded the area. Farther to my right, I spied the great wall that circled the manor property.

"Keep moving." The man prodded my shoulder, and I cried out loud as the piercing pain ripped through my stabbed shoulder like shattered glass.

Blood dribbled down my arm, and every step grew sluggish. The world tilted around me, and I stumbled in a zigzag line.

"Please." I turned to the man. "Will you help me? I don't want to die."

"Help you? A fucking wolf who eats humans? You deserve everything coming your way." He hissed the words, and I glanced back at the manor and its arched windows, but not a soul looked out to witness this atrocity. Where did the rest of the royal family live?

Ahead of me, I found the priestess, yawning as if I'd inconvenienced her. *Bitch.* Two more guards stood on either

198

side of her. And Santos was there too, unconscious, tied to a tree by the neck as if he were a dog. I shivered. What had they done to him?

When I laid eyes on the guillotine nearby, I lost my breath. Who the hell had one of those devices in their backyard? The blade looked rusty from lack of use—or was the metal stained with blotches of blood!? She was officially insane, because it meant she'd used this before. How many innocents had lost their heads? I shuddered and recoiled, picturing myself decapitated.

A flicker at the edge of the woods caught my eye. A fox jumped over a log and sprinted out of there. Exactly what I had to do.

My muscles exploded with a violent motion, and I darted toward a cluster of trees in the direction of the front gates.

The guard snatched my arm and yanked me backward. But I tripped over my feet and crashed onto my butt, every inch of me screaming with pain.

"Get up," he snarled.

"No. I've done nothing wrong. You're the monsters here, killing innocent people."

The man dragged me across the grass, my body hurting with every jounce, and he dumped me near the priestess.

"Oh dear," she mocked. "She actually thinks she's a person."

The priestess grabbed my hair and pulled me up. I staggered upright, gritting my teeth, and was sick of being treated like a nobody. No wonder wolves hated us if this was how the guards treated them.

I held myself upright, despite my legs shaking and my vision wavering from the lack of blood, yet I held her glare.

"You will never be anything but a fucking bitch," I shouted.

She laughed, and rage bubbled in my chest. The earlier

connection to my wolf had vanished back in the cell. Didn't matter. I steadied my balance and head-butted her in the face. Sure, the pain ricocheted through my skull and down to my shoulder, but I bit down on my tongue until the throbbing stabs passed.

Her lower lip busted open, and she clasped her mouth, her eyes wide.

"I'm proud of what I am," I roared. "Scum like you can never take that away."

The guard tackled me from behind, both of us hitting the ground. Air gushed from my lungs, and I hollered for the injustice of how much damage the leader had done to Terra.

"Set her up. Now!" She held a tissue to her bloody lip.

"You deserve so much worse," I said.

I bucked against the guard, but another guard joined, taking my injured arm, twisting it so much I howled in pain. They pushed me toward the guillotine, and I wedged a leg up against the wooden frame, stopping them from pushing me closer. My heart raced and fire seared my brain as I gawked at the open basket where my head would roll. Sickness plunged into my gut.

Someone kicked the back of my knee, and I collapsed, crying, unable to stop.

A hand grabbed the back of my neck and pressed me forward.

"No!" I screamed.

Somewhere behind us, thundering footfalls struck the ground, growing louder and closer.

The grip holding me eased, and I scrambled away from the monstrous contraption, but the guard clasped my wrist. I pried at his iron fingers that refused to budge.

"What is it now?" the priestess shouted.

I stared up at the four guards marching toward us through the trees from the direction of the front gate. But the moment they emerged with someone grasped between two of them, ice filled my veins.

"Oryn?" I whispered.

He was naked, and bleeding cuts dotted his body. My chest clenched, and I clawed at the guard's arms.

"Who is this?" She stormed closer.

"Priestess, we found this shifter on our land in his wolf form. But he was no match for us." The men stood proudly, with their chests sticking out, chins high.

"Yeah, big men when it's four against one," I blurted out.

Oryn's head lifted, his gaze on mine, and when he winked, a newfound energy filled me. The men were coming for me, and I bounced in my boots. Oryn getting caught wasn't an accident. I'd seen him take down ferocious wolves, so four guards were nothing. But they shouldn't have come and placed themselves in danger.

"This is your doing," the priestess said. "You're calling more of your kind onto my land." The priestess scoffed and turned to Oryn. "Bring him to me." She dug into her pocket and took out a fabric pouch. "Shifters will be extinct soon enough. You two are just leaving earlier."

"What's in the pouch?" I asked as my thoughts flew to the poisoned river.

Her smirk left me terrified. "A little something I ordered from the Darkwoods. Did you know you can find almost anything there? Disgusting place, but sometimes a necessity."

When the guard kicked Oryn's leg, he dropped to his knees, but his hands snapped free the tie binding his wrists behind his back.

My breath froze in my chest.

He leaped to his feet as she snatched a pinch of whatever was in her bag and blew it into his face.

Oryn flinched backward and sneezed. Then his eyes rolled back and he slumped onto his side, unmoving.

"Oryn!" I drove my heel into the guard's foot and broke free. I ran around the guillotine and slid to my knees next to him, cupping his face with my good hand. "Wake up." Listening to his chest, his heartbeat was present, but faint.

I glanced up to the priestess. "What did you do?"

She shrugged, tucking away her pouch into a pocket of her dress. "Just a little something that will shut down his organs. It's the most humane way to do it. He's not suffering."

I rocked on the spot. "You're killing him for no reason." I reached down and placed my palm on his chest, driving my power into his. The buzzing tingled down my arm. I'd done it before, so it *had* to work now. I held the priestess' gaze to keep her distracted.

"Is that how you poisoned the water in the Den?"

"Smart girl. The toxin in the stream will turn the beasts against each other until they're all dead. Then my job is done. And I'll claim their territory and expand Terra. We are the original beings. Pure and free of imperfections."

"How can you sleep at night? Knowing you'll be the cause of the mass extinction of a race?"

A guard shoved me in the back.

"She's doing something to him. Her hand is glowing."

I turned, but a fist collided with my cheek. Stars danced before me, and I collapsed onto my back. My world danced, and voices spoke, but nothing made sense. Not when my head vibrated and felt as if someone had ripped out my jaw. How in the world did men keep fighting after getting punched?

Hands grabbed my waist and lifted me to my feet, but everything in my sight was duplicated.

"Set her up and let's finish this. I'm starving." The priestess patted down her dress, brushing off dead leaves.

He gripped my arm tight, and I winced from the pain in my shoulder as he dragged me to the guillotine.

"Let me go." A quick look behind me as I stumbled forward, and Oryn hadn't shifted. But the other shifters were coming, and I had to buy them time, so I addressed the priestess.

"I can offer you herbs that will heal almost anything. Maybe you'd prefer a rejuvenation mixture for younger skin. No one else in the seven realms can make such an offer."

"Stop wasting my time," she said.

"Let me show you what I can do," I pleaded as I pulled my free hand from the guard and gripped my wounded shoulder, anything to ease the spasms jolting down my arm. I fought the desperate urge to cry and beg for mercy. Oryn, Nero, and Dagen. They risked their lives to safe me. And I couldn't allow them to die.

"Everyone comes to my store for a reason," I began, my head still buzzing. "I've found a plant that, when placed on sore knees, will eradicate joint pain. My herbs work."

"Enough!" Her lips twisted. "Do you think I'd use a potion from a shifter?" Her nose wrinkled, and she turned to the guard. "Do this, already."

When he placed a hand on me, I kicked him in the shin.

"I'm not the enemy here."

He didn't react, but he squeezed my arm so hard it hurt. "Stop squirming, or I'll give you something to *really* scream about." He cocked a brow and stared at me with his beady pig eyes.

"You'll never touch me." I kneed him in the balls and stumbled back toward Oryn, but other guards crowded around and grasped me. I coiled in on myself, cradling my injured shoulder tight against my side. Despair squeezed my heart. I'd finally found three special men and I was about to lose them.

But I'd lived with darkness for years after Grandma died,

enough to last an eternity. She raised me to stand up for myself, so I lifted my chin, ready to fight.

When a howl echoed around us, my heart leaped.

A flurry of bodies dashed around us, and only one guard remained by my side. The others hovered near the priestess, their long knives drawn. I peered through the chaos, fighting my blurred vision.

More guards rushed from the manor.

My breaths raced, and I kept staring at Oryn, willing him to get up. But he didn't move.

A grunt came from farther behind the guillotine.

I twisted, to see an army of at least a dozen wolves charging toward us, led by Dagen in his dark fur.

Dagen. Yes. I love you so much.

I kicked the guard holding on to me. Sidestepping around him, I staggered to Oryn. *Don't let it be too late.*

Behind me, an explosion of snarls erupted. I jerked toward the clash of wolves and guards tangled in a brawl. The guard who'd been holding me had joined the fight. I had to believe Dagen knew what he was doing. Had the shifters spent the morning retrieving wolf members not affected by the poison to rescue me?

Crouched near Oryn, I placed a palm on his chest. "Come back to me."

I ignored the priestess retreating along the path, the cries and whimpers nearby, because my heart tore at the blood being spilled because of a crazy woman.

With my eyes shut, I refocused on my central core, the fizzing energy, and compelled it down my arms. The energy shot to my hands, and I snapped open my eyes to find the web-like charge hopping across Oryn's torso.

Still no response. I listened to his heart. Alive. But for how long? And why wasn't my touch working?

I staggered to my feet and stumbled after the priestess, who rushed away like a coward while her men fell.

"What herbs did you put in your pouch?" I demanded to know.

She waved me away as if I were a pest in her sight.

Except right then, my veins were alight, and I refused to lose any of my men. I snatched her fingers and twisted them back.

She shrieked and moved too fast for me to see her holding a weapon in her other hand. She swung the blade in my direction and plunged it into my chest.

I screamed and fell to my knees. The agonizing pain paralyzed me. Every twitch I made had me bellowing. Blood poured out.

"Now you will die like the animal you are." The priestess shoved me aside as she ran toward the manor.

Crashing onto the ground, I cried from the agony, from losing my life, and for never seeing those I loved ever again.

CHAPTER 22

a war raged around me. Wolf against human. And I lay on the grass, where the ground seemed to sway beneath me. Each inhale was a painful gasp, as if my ribs were crushed. I clasped my chest, the knife still embedded in me.

Tears flooded my eyes, but I kept looking into the same heavens I used to pray toward. Prayed for finding the right partner and having a family, expanding my store to produce healing potions to help anyone in need, not just for those living in Terra.

But did any of that matter if I died?

A tremor ran through me. I'd lost everything. Death crowded the edges of my mind, coming for me. I regretted so many things. I should have dug deeper into what Grandma had meant about my parents' demise. Discovered her secret compartment and letter earlier. Then I could have somehow avoided this ending.

A shadow fell over me, but I didn't care who'd come to finish me. I could barely move.

"Little lamb." Nero's voice was strained, and he dropped to his knees. "I'm removing the blade."

"No!" I managed. "I'll bleed too much." Were my words slurring?

Blood streaked his cheeks, and a deep gash ran down the side of his face, droplets falling against my skin. The wound seemed to almost knit back together before my eyes. Oh hell, how fast did these wolves heal?

But how many wolves and people had died because of the priestess?

"Go," I stammered.

He laid a hand against my collarbone. "Don't you dare leave us! Hold on." His eyes glistened and right then, his genuine love for me shone through his actions, his words, his warmth.

He yanked the knife out, the sucking sound sickening to my ears.

I yelled, my body thrashing at the terrifying pain stabbing me.

Nero placed his palms against my wound. "Transform, little lamb."

His words floated through my brain, torn away by the torture owning me. I cried out.

"I read the letter from your grandma. You're part hunter. Change and you will heal quicker. You're only part shifter and need the wolf side to help you."

"I... I." Nothing made sense when it felt as if someone had ripped me apart.

Nero's lips were on mine, stealing my breath. Something warm dripped on my face, my neck, and into my mouth. His blood.

A surge of energy flashed over me, and my skin prickled. My insides stretched. Each exhale was a knife slicing me. I writhed and a violent scream tore past my mouth. Bones cracked. My heart banged in my ears.

I was dying.

"Stop fighting it." Nero's voice found me, but my vision had darkened.

"Nero!" I called for him, but moving my arms now seemed an impossibility.

Energy jolted along my skin, and I gulped for air.

"Open your eyes," he said.

I did, and gawked at Nero kneeling next to me. The forest had grown sharper in color and focus, as it had back in the dungeon. Grunts, whines, and the dull impact of punches reached me, each sound precise.

But the earlier stabbing in my chest had eased, and the agony had disappeared. How?

Nero rubbed my head. "You look beautiful in your silver fur. And it looks like you've healed faster than I've ever seen anyone do."

Fur! I opened my mouth to protest, but a yelp came out. I froze. Was that me? Whispers murmured calmness into my ears.

I scrambled to my feet... all four of them, scanning the area. So many sounds hit me—from the battle, to the river in the distance, to the songs of birds. The smell of blood engulfed me.

The piercing pain in my chest came and went, paralyzing me on the spot when it shook me to the core.

Nero was there, his arms around my torso. "I've got you. Now you need to run from here. Let us finish this once and for all." He patted my rump and nudged me toward the front gates.

But I couldn't move when I'd just turned into a wolf. The realization locked me in place, not a muscle moved, not even the panic jammed in my chest stirred me.

Nero rushed into battle, and mid-launch, his body shifted with the grace of an eagle swooping through the air. Within moments, he landed on his paws, his white fur fluttering as he charged two guards holding down a wolf.

Bodies lay everywhere, both human and wolf, and it killed me. Dread punched me in the gut, hollow and barren, reminding me of the stories I'd read about the different races in Haven fighting to the death. That was why the world had been divided into seven realms. To create peace—the opposite of what the priestess had done.

Toward the manor, I spotted her, holding her skirt and running into the building. Before I could stop myself, I went after her, each step slow. Every now and then, my shoulder stung as if someone tossed boiling water over it. Obviously, healing as a wolf took time... A luxury I didn't have.

I pushed one leg forward, and then another, gaining speed.

A dark wolf blur whizzed past me and thundered through the courtyard.

Oryn?

My legs refused to fall into a rhythm, and I stumbled into a tree. Heavens, how did anyone walk on four paws? Okay, one at a time.

Someone screeched from the manor, and I sped up. The moment I entered the cobblestone yard, I gasped.

Six guards cornered Oryn, while the priestess held a long, thin knife in one hand, poised in a striking pose above her shoulder.

"Grab him and hold him down," she yelled.

My stomach somersaulted, and a guttural snarl rolled through me, shaking me. No one touched my shifter. A sense of possessiveness claimed me.

All gazes turned in my direction, and I lunged at the

priestess, hating what she'd done to Terra, the fear she'd inflicted, and the merciless deaths.

She whirled around, her blade pointed at me.

Everything happened too fast, and I swore the wolf side of me pushed forward, reaffirming we had this. To trust her.

Nearby, Oryn jumped into his own assault, battling the guards. But one turned toward me.

Just out of reach of the priestess, I swung around her in a wide arc, then ricocheted against the wall for leverage. The pain increased in waves, but I drove it back. I twisted and pivoted midair, hurling myself toward her.

She jerked around as I crashed into her, my mouth latching into her neck. We both fell to the ground, her blade falling, and me biting down.

Her cries meant nothing.

Blood hit my tongue.

Kill. My wolf bellowed. For my parents' deaths. For Dagen's brother. For Oryn's pack members. And for the countless other wolves and humans.

A guard charged and kicked me in the ribs.

I crumpled, writhing, my pain deep, stabbing and burning.

He circled closer, his knife ready.

My blood painted the cobblestones as I teetered upright. Exhaustion crashed over me.

"Kill it," the priestess shouted as she climbed to her feet, crimson coating her neck and gown.

I growled. No more backing away or feeling sorry for myself. I'd fight for what I believed in, stand up to the enemy.

Right when the guard lunged, I ducked and looped around him.

I bit into his arm, the one clasping the weapon, and tore through bone.

He grunted and collapsed to his knees.

Something flashed into the courtyard in my peripheral vision.

More guards? I spun to see two wolves! Nero rushing to Oryn's aid, while Dagen slammed into the back of the guard I'd just bitten.

Now it was just me and the priestess.

I inched closer, my head low. Short, sharp throbbing settled over my shoulder blade, as if someone poked me with a fire stick.

But no more hesitation. I'd heal if I survived.

When she ran across the yard to a set of doors, her gown swooshing around her feet, I leaped after her and head-butted the back of her knees.

She tripped and hit the ground face-first.

Oryn's black wolf burst free from the scuffle and flew past me toward the priestess.

She swung in his direction, cowering, her arms covering her head.

Oryn attacked. Teeth slashed her neck, blood spurting. Her pleas and cries echoed, as did the hungry snarls and ripping of flesh.

I turned away, unable to watch the bloodshed, kicking myself for ever thinking I was capable of such a kill.

Maybe that came with time, considering I hadn't even gotten the whole walking on four legs thing perfected yet.

When someone brushed my arm, I flinched and whirled.

Oryn was there, blood matted in his fur and around his mouth, but he rubbed against me, releasing a low grumble. Behind him lay the priestess, unmoving, her legs twisted at wrong angles, her head facing the sky with dead eyes.

I should have cheered, but I couldn't bring myself to celebrate. A life lost was still a wasted soul.

Nero closed in, his white fur tarnished, both shifters close.

Guards lay strewn across the ground, dead.

Dagen approached me without hesitation in his step. A wave of joy flooded me at knowing my three shifters remained safe and by my side.

Dagen nuzzled my arm when more wolves entered the courtyard and fanned out as a protective army.

Oryn broke into a piercing howl, and everyone else raised their heads, unleashing a cry of triumph. My wolf simmered in my chest, and I tilted my chin up, my contribution streaming past my throat.

Our songs intertwined, blending into the most incredible tune. For the first time since losing my parents and Grandma, I no longer felt alone.

CHAPTER 23

I turned to my three wolves traipsing alongside me as we strode in animal form toward the border between Terra and the Den. Oryn carried my bag in his mouth, the one with the ingredients to remedy the toxic river. He'd killed the priestess, done what I probably couldn't have. But he'd had his own reasons for finishing her off, and I couldn't deny the world was a better place without her.

Walking through the woods was a million times easier this way, light and swift. I was a wolf! With a gorgeous silver coat, too.

Behind us, a dozen wolves trailed; a few carried their fallen warriors in human form on their backs. My heart bled to know their families had lost a member. These hunters had given their lives to eliminate the monster ruling Terra. Who knew how the royal family would react to discovering her dead. But we weren't hanging around to find out, the priority was still helping Oryn's pack.

I stepped over foliage, the prickly forest floor not hurting my paws. What amazed me even more was how quickly my body had healed from the knife wounds in my chest and shoulder once I'd changed into my wolf. Heavens... Me, a shifter. I couldn't believe it.

We made a small detour to Bee's place and dropped off Santos. He'd fainted from a knock to the head. But other than a few cuts, he was fine, which made me all kinds of happy. Now he had to keep a low profile for a few weeks.

At the border, several wolves worked as a team and pushed two dead logs over the wolfsbane shrubs, flattening the plants. They'd created a narrow passage in no time.

Their strategy told me so many things. Like how the shifters could have easily crossed into Terra whenever they'd wanted, but they hadn't because they'd had no intention of fighting or killing us. The real maniac was the priestess, and just knowing she was out of the picture eased the heaviness from my shoulders. Sure, the danger wasn't gone, but it was a reprieve to catch my breath and work out what I'd do next without her death sentence for me breathing down my back.

Besides, I now had a family to consider.

Wolves crossed over into the Den, followed by Oryn and Nero. Once Dagen and I passed through, he stood in my path, blocking me.

He shifted into his human form, his sizzling energy caressing me, and, as if my wolf sensed the change, already I felt her retreat inside me and vanish. My legs wobbled and I fell on all fours, fur retreating from all over my body, my limbs shortening. But, this time, the agony of the transformation no longer hurt but felt like I'd pulled off a raincoat stuck to my skin with sweat.

Dagen lifted himself to his feet and took my hand into his, drawing me to my feet.

I glanced at the rest of the pack, heading on toward the open field, while we remained beneath the shadows of the pines.

"Now that we're alone, I need to apologize," he said.

I shook my head. "No, you don't. For what?"

With a kiss to the back of my hand, he drew me closer, our naked bodies plastered together. "For doubting you and scaring you earlier. And mostly for calling you 'vile.'"

My mouth opened, but he pressed his mouth against mine, and my world faded beneath his heat.

"You are the most beautiful person I've ever met," he said, our foreheads touching. "I want you in my life, if you'll have me."

I stared into his gaze, lost, and my heart drummed with the excitement that Dagen had offered himself to me. "Hell, yeah. There was never any doubt in my mind."

He laughed. "I know. Just wanted to hear it from your sweet voice."

A howl came from across the open field, and my thoughts flew to danger. I snapped around, only to find the wolves strolling, while Nero stared back at us. I released a long exhale when Dagen took my hand, and we hurried to catch up with the pack.

By the time we reached the top of a cliff near the river, we stopped. I was out of breath, but, then again, we'd been rushing up and down slopes.

Oryn transformed with such ease, it looked graceful to me. He approached me. "Sharlot, the river flows from here, and it's the best location to ensure we cleanse the source of the river."

I nodded, but exhaustion washed through me. What I wouldn't give to sleep a whole week. Cuts and bruises littered my body, blood still dribbling from the wound on my chest, but it amazed me how little pain remained. No wonder wolves kept fighting with their endless stamina. Yet my job here wasn't complete.

I crouched near the edge of the river and Oryn brought me my bag.

"What can I do?" he asked.

I collected the parcel I'd prepared in the store and turned to him. Desperation brimmed in his eyes. "Bring me an affected wolf so we can try to see if this will work."

He nodded and vanished behind me, past where the other wolves stood.

In all honesty, if this didn't prove the solution, I was lost. I'd scanned Grandma's book and no other cure offered a solution to the poisoning. The priestess had said she'd bought the toxin from the Darkwoods realm. Heavens, that could be anything, and with her dead, we'd never find out. My stomach knotted, but I had to think positive.

Pulling out a bowl from the bag, I bent toward the current and scooped water into it. Around me, nature was at its most glorious, the sun descending while its golden hues lit up the pines and glistened across the river.

I lifted the pouch with prepared herbs and opened the tied cord. With no idea how much was needed to cleanse such a large volume of water, I'd tripled the quantities. But rivers were enormous, and what if the cure washed away before the wolves drank it from the main pool were Oryn and I had hid in the waterfall? He had said that was where the wolves often drank as the waters were shallow and the stream moved slower. That gave the toxins time to collect in one place. That was why only the wolves in a certain part of the Den had been affected over a specific period. The poison washed downstream. And what if my quantities weren't enough?

"Time to do this," I whispered to myself before pouring the contents into the bowl. They floated across the surface of the water, and I placed my palms over them, and a snap of energy rolled down my arm. It zapped out from my fingertips, infusing the contents. Never stopping, I imagined wolves drinking it and healing at once.

A wave of dizziness captured me, and I stopped. Okay, I'd pushed myself, so I climbed to my feet and tossed the amplified water from the bowl out across the river.

The moment it touched the water, a sizzling spark snapped across the surface, as if it had been struck by lightning.

Someone gasped behind me, and Nero was there, whispering in my ear. "What was that?"

"Hopefully, the solution to help Oryn's pack."

An aggressive snarl erupted, and I spotted Oryn and Dagen carrying a thrashing wolf. Dagen held a hand clamped around its mouth.

I snatched my bowl and filled it with the cleansed water, then rushed toward them. "Put him down," I said. "We need him to drink this."

Oryn held his head. Jaws snapped. The animal growled, his throat rumbling, saliva frothing at the sides of his mouth.

I leaned closer and poured the solution into his jaw. He shook, spat it out, spraying all of us.

"Keep trying," Oryn said.

Once again, I dribbled more down his throat, and that time he swallowed. So I kept feeding him mouthfuls.

But when the wolf's eyes rolled upward, I said, "Release him."

And we all stepped back as the afflicted wolf shuddered.

I held my breath, and I reached over, grabbing Oryn's hand.

Within moments, the animal's body trembled. One leg kicked outward, stretching, then the others, his skin elongating, ears shortening.

"Yes, it's working," I called out.

No one moved and the four of us stared as the former wolf now resembled a female who had to be in her forties.

She glanced up at us, panic gripping her features. "Oryn?"

Her voice squeaked. "What's happening?"

He squatted near her and helped her up. "Nexy, you are safe now."

Joy beamed in my heart because it meant the remedy had worked.

Nero was by my side and lifted me into his arms, spinning me. "Little lamb, you did it."

I laughed, unable to stop, because for the first time in too long, something had gone right. "Now we get all the affected wolves to drink the water."

Oryn reached me as Nero dropped me to my feet. "I can't thank you enough."

"You owe me nothing," I said.

"Yes, I do." He reached over and kissed me. "I owe you my life, my future, my love."

It hurt to smile so much and having three men stare at me with admiration left me jittering with excitement.

"Me, too," Nero added.

"And me." Dagen squeezed my hand.

"Each and every one of you are mine," I said.

Nero burst out laughing. "So now you know what we were talking about earlier, hey?"

I nudged him in the gut. "It feels incredible. But what now?" I asked.

"Well," Oryn began, "I will get as many of my pack to drink the water as I can."

"My wolves and I will come with you to help," Nero piped up.

"Me, too." Dagen squared his shoulders. "We do this now."

Oryn stared at me, his eyes softening, almost calling me over to leap into his arms. "Dagen, how about you stay with Scarlet? Mend her wounds. We shouldn't leave her alone until we know all the wolves are healed."

Dagen stared at me with an evil grin and nodded. He enveloped me in an embrace.

Within moments, everyone took off in different directions, and by the time Dagen and I entered the house, a strange sensation filled me. This place had changed my life for eternity. If I'd never fallen over that cliff, or met these shifters, would I have lived my entire life never knowing the real me? Never comprehending that wolf blood ran through my veins? Or about the priestess torturing her people and wolves endlessly?

I turned to Dagen, who collected me into his arms.

"Finally, I have you all to myself," he purred in my ears, and I trembled with desire. The emotion hit me so hard, my knees weakened.

"So, you think this will work? All of us together when we live so far apart?"

Dagen picked me up in his arms, holding me like a baby, and carried me toward the living room where I'd woken up when I first arrived in the house. He kicked the door shut behind us.

"We may each rule territories and live in different places, but we also share a huge house, deeper in the Den. So we could all bunk up there." He winked, and I couldn't stop smiling.

"Well, I was thinking I might lie low until things settle down in Terra."

"You're not going anywhere until we know it's safe. You went off alone to your store in the night, so from now on one of us will accompany you. And that's not negotiable. You'll stay with us until then."

This was happening… Us together. Though what about my shop? I'd have to wait until they appointed a new leader of Terra.

But when Dagen lowered his lips to mine, I forgot every worry and let myself float on his desire.

He lowered me to the rug in front of the fireplace and hovered over me.

I chewed on my lower lip, my whole body buzzing with anticipation. Yes, everything had happened at tornado speed, and for once I felt at peace. I understood the role I played, and rather than questioning my attraction to the shifters, now... I craved them, and I experienced no hesitation in taking what I desired.

"You going to keep staring at me?" I asked. "Or are you going to give me what you've kept from me for too long?"

A sexy growl rolled from Dagen's throat, and I shivered at the huge man lying over the top of me, the hunger in his eyes, the hardness pressing against my stomach.

"You have no idea what you've unleashed, do you?"

I shrugged and giggled. "I'm ready for everything you've got."

Dagen crawled down my body, his tongue on me, flicking my nipples and taking mock bites of my flesh.

On my back, I moaned, unable to believe my luck that I'd end up with not one amazing man, but three.

"Hey," Dagen said as he lightly slapped the side of my thigh. "You're still in my mind, so focus on your man right here." He smirked and widened my legs, his head lowering. "Your scent is intoxicating."

"I think we'll always be connected." I smiled while a shiver ran the length of my body at seeing this huge, powerful man kneeling between my thighs. He slid his tongue along my silkiness, stealing my breath.

Air gasped from my lungs as I moaned.

His mouth latched on to my clit, sucking, pulling at my inner lips. Thinking became impossible.

I raised my pelvis, rocking back and forth with the sexy

rhythm of his passion. Writhing beneath him, my body responded to Dagen, sparking into a blaze. I swooned, lost in a world where I intended to remain forever.

"Yes. Oh, shit." I shuddered, my body caught in its own ecstasy.

"That's it. Rub your sexy pussy in my face. Cum in my mouth." He latched on to my sensitive folds, sucking so hard, I lost it.

I cried out as he claimed my body. I belonged to him. He owned me.

My muscles tensed as he licked over my entrance. He pushed me open wider and his tongue fucked me. His thumb rubbed my clit.

Heat burned through my body. My nipples pebbled so tight, they hurt, and I needed more. One last roll over my nub, and I fell apart.

A scream streamed from my throat as an orgasm rocked through me.

"Daaagen!" I screamed his name.

His tongue was relentless and licked up every drop.

I puddled, boneless and panting, onto the floor, while he lifted himself, his mouth and chin glistening. His smile belonged to the happiest man in the world.

"Come here." He sat on the rug, stretching out his legs on either side of me, so I got onto my stomach and crawled toward him.

I straddled him, and he curled my legs around his hips.

"I like to watch," he said as he pulled my hips closer. With his cock in his hand, he ran his tip along my slit.

"Yes. Let me feel all of you." I leaned back on my hands to hold myself up so I could see.

He pushed into me, and I gasped as he reached and placed my legs over his shoulders. "Now hold on, little one." With his hands behind him for support, he lifted his hips, deepening his penetration. Spreading me wider. Heavens... he was huge.

I lifted my butt, and he ground into me in circles, touching parts no one ever had before, his gaze lowered to between my legs.

"Hell."

"That's right." He laughed and plunged into me, his hips raised off the floor slightly, and together we moved. He slammed into me so forcefully, I trembled from each euphoric thrust.

His face held the most intense expression as he fucked me. Damn, the swear words now rolled in my mind as if I were a sailor.

I shook, moaning, loving that Dagen forced me so wide.

He glided an arm around my back and drew me closer, his cock still buried deep inside me. "You're so beautiful. I plan to fuck you until exhaustion takes both of us."

"Challenge accepted." I curled my legs under me and slid up and down.

With his hands on my hips, he moved me faster over his shaft.

My breaths raced.

"Love how your body tightens around me."

The moment he leaned closer and grasped a nipple into his mouth, I mewled. Tightness coiled in my stomach, and I trembled with the orgasm shaking me.

"That's it," he groaned. "Squeeze my cock with your pussy." His eyes rolled back as I exploded and he pulsed inside me at the same time.

I collapsed into his arms, our bodies sweaty, hearts racing, and I couldn't stop smiling. He held me hard and whispered, "I think I'm falling for you so fast, it scares me."

Pulling back, I cupped his face and kissed his lips. "There's nothing to be afraid of. You are everything. All three of you own my heart. And a week ago that would have terrified me. Now, I can't imagine my life any different."

He leaned close and kissed me, soft and passionate, his fingers digging into my flesh as if he couldn't get close enough. And I knew the terror of thinking something was too good to be true. But damn it, after everything we'd gone through, the universe had forced us together because we were meant to be. Now and for eternity.

CHAPTER 24

SIX MONTHS LATER

*R*eds and yellows streaked the early morning sky. I leaned a hip into the wooden railing while drinking a warm cup of chamomile tea. A cool breeze swished through my hair and ruffled my long slip-dress, bringing with it the chill from the White Peak Mountains in the distance.

For months, I'd been living with my shifters in the middle of the Den in a massive two-story wooden house. Here I thought hunters slept outdoors and ate whatever they caught. How wrong I'd been. Most packs I visited had huts and gardens and an established society. Plus, each pack had embraced me within seconds without a single hesitation. I guessed it helped that they'd smelled my wolf side, and I felt as if I belonged, as this was my home and had always been. I'd just had to find my way here.

I stared down at the green field below as a white rabbit hopped past, while birds squawked in the nearby pines. Yep, if heaven were to exist in all of Haven, the Den was it. Shifters had been smart to scare intruders away because they'd kept their simple and pure life untainted by others, who'd want to cut down trees and hunt the animals to extinction.

A tightness squeezed around my waist, and I held my breath until it passed, rubbing my huge belly.

Another surprise... I'd become pregnant and, as a part shifter, it meant my term only lasted six months. Damn, I couldn't wait to pop, because I'd had enough of waddling and resembling a walrus. Then I'd visit Terra again. For the past two months, the shifters had insisted I stay in the Den, near our house, protected. I had more than just me to care for, but our unborn child.

Back in Terra, the royals had appointed a distant cousin in the position of priestess, and, to date, she'd kept quiet, from what I'd heard from Bee and Santos. The new priestess in Terra had kept low. There had been no attacks on locals or neighboring races in Terra. Though she hadn't lifted the insane laws about it being illegal to leave Terra or to have others visiting the place, either. Yet there were fewer guards patrolling. A win on my end, so my shifters had been spending time there, rebuilding my shop. And in my state, I wasn't going anywhere.

I've been catching up with Bee and Santos every few weeks since leaving Terra.

Except, last time I saw Santos, he said Bee kept going back and forth from home to the White Peaks, but she'd hadn't returned home for two weeks now. And that worried me. Was she okay?

The ache in my lower back deepened, and I paced along the veranda to distract myself from the pain. Past the bench and small picnic table and chairs. It was hard enough being pregnant, let alone as a shifter, as I had zero idea what to expect.

"Little lamb." Nero joined me outside, holding a pair of

MILA YOUNG

slippers in his hand. "You shouldn't be wandering around barefoot."

"I'm fine. It cools me down, as I'm burning up."

He cocked an eyebrow and dropped the slippers in front of me. Just as I stepped into them, Dagen emerged with a plate of egg toast, just the way I'd taught them to make it, while Oryn followed soon after with a blanket.

My men. They pampered me at every turn, and, for the past two weeks, none had left my side, insisting they didn't want to miss the birth of our child.

There was no way of knowing whose specific kid it would be, but that didn't matter because we were one family. And Oryn had already carved every wooden toy under the sun, ready to become a father. Dagen took my hand and led me to the chair and placed the plate of food in front of me.

"A girl could get used to this kind of spoiling," I said.

They surrounded me, each placing a hand on my stomach, and Dagen leaned in closer, stealing a kiss. "You grow more beautiful every day. We love you so much."

"Have a seat," Nero offered, "and I'll rub your feet."

"Well, when you put it that way." I laughed, just as something cramped in my lower stomach and I gasped, clutching onto their arms.

A pop sounded and warmth spread down my legs.

"Her water broke," Oryn called out for the entire forest to hear.

All my men jumped about, as if suddenly the world was coming to an end. Oryn rushed into the house for who-knew-what. Nero darted to the end of the veranda, screaming at someone to call the midwife, while Dagen's eyes widened, his cheeks blanching.

"I'm going to become a dad!" His words wavered, and I swore he'd be the first one to faint. For some reason, I'd pictured it being Nero.

I held on to his arm, and he held me close. "Looks like it," I said.

We moved indoors, me in slow motion like a great whale. The weight of the baby, now that my water had broken, felt like a boulder pressing down onto my pelvis. In the bedroom, our new bed stretched across the entire length of the room, with enough space for us all to sleep together. After all, wolves always huddled, so it made perfect sense that we stayed close.

Some nights we had insane sex marathons and the men enjoyed watching as I spent time with each one of them, and it turned me on to no end.

A sudden contraction hit, and I cried out, clasping my belly. I bent over, grasping on to the edge of the dressing table to ease the ache. Unable to move or breathe as the pain lanced through me, my knees shook until the contraction finally subsided.

Dagen rubbed my back. "Take deep, slow breaths."

"Nero!" he yelled. "Where's the midwife?"

Oryn returned with an armful of towels and a bucket of what I imagined was hot water. He'd paid the closest attention to the instructions from the midwife on what to do when labor hit.

"Let's get her on the bed," he said.

Together, they guided me onto the mattress as Nero rushed into the room.

"The midwife is coming."

Catching my breath as another contraction eased, I panted. Oryn patted my brow with a moist towel.

"Looks like we're about to have a baby," I said. And around me, all three men stared at me with awe in their eyes, and, considering this was a first for me, I couldn't be happier to share this experience with them.

When the next contraction came, faster and more intense,

MILA YOUNG

I screamed. "Fuck! I think it's happening." I was being ripped apart, starting at my groin and radiating to every fiber of my being.

All three men jumped about, dashing in every direction as if lost, and, at one moment, they all ran out of the room. I couldn't help but laugh in between the cries of pain. Even breathing was difficult, and I panted through the contractions like the midwife had told me. The muscles in my womb cramped down so hard I couldn't do anything. Everything in me pushed down to my cervix, the pressure heightening like I was going to burst apart.

Heavens, this was really happening.

* * *

For the first time since giving birth, I'd left the Den, and returning to Terra brought back familiar memories, both scary and comforting.

The moment I stepped into the refurbished Get Your Herb On, I gasped with excitement and clapped. There was a counter in an L-shape, with a new section dedicated to taste-testing, as two jugs sat there with multiple cups. The shelves on the back wall had mirrors behind them, giving the whole place a bigger appearance. To my right stood a display cabinet stuffed with ceramic teapots. They had to have been imported from other realms. And nearby was a small round table with four seats. Was that for serving customers tea? What a fabulous idea.

Oryn brushed past my elbow. "What do you think?"

"I can't believe how incredible this is." I turned to face him. He cradled our little Alexy, who stuffed Oryn's pinky finger in her mouth as she suckled it. At just one month old, she already sported a full head of dark hair, and she had the brightest blue eyes.

228

"Did you see that?" He pointed his chin to the wall behind me. I stepped deeper into the shop and turned around. Between the windows hung my painting of Grandma in the woods.

My throat thickened, and I wiped my eyes. "I don't even know what to say."

Dagen entered the store, holding our second joy in his arms, Jay, named after Dagen's brother. That little boy slept through anything, and sometimes the hardest part was waking him up to eat.

"Have you checked behind the counter? I built something for you."

"Oh, really?" I hurried back there and found a set of three long, shallow drawers built into the counter. I pulled out one and inside lay at least two dozen compartments, each labeled with various herbs, ready and waiting to be filled.

Dagen was next to me. "I found an old herb book and tried to add as many of the names as I could find."

"This is fantastic." I leaned against his side and stole a kiss before placing a peck on Jay's forehead.

"Hey, don't forget to look in the storage room. I had a hand in this, too," Nero said, holding our third munchkin, blowing her raspberries. We'd called her Autumn after my grandma, and I swore, when she looked at me, I saw an old soul in her eyes. She rarely cried and laughed more than anything.

Within such a small space of time, I'd gone from being alone and losing everything to gaining a family. Now there were seven of us. I adored every single one, and I doubted our lives would ever be the same again.

"I love you all so much," I said, pressing my palms to my heart, my eyes watering. "You don't understand how much this means to me."

"Oh, we know," Nero teased. "Now check out the back room."

"Okay, okay." I strode to the back, unable to believe this place was mine, or how handy my men were. I pushed open the door to a darkened room, and the moment I stepped inside, Bee leaped out from behind the door.

"Surprise." She jumped into my arms, driving us both backward.

I yelped, my heart soaring into my throat. "Oh, crap."

"Girl, did you think you'd keep me away from seeing your little ones?" Bee broke free and stared at me. "Wow. You're a mom. I still can't believe it."

"How long have you been hiding?" To see her after I'd been so worried she had gone missing in the mountains eased my concern. "Where have you been these past few weeks? Santos and I have been worried sick."

"You won't believe what happened to me! I have lots to tell you. But not now. I'll tell you later, okay?"

I nodded and turned to the men. "Did you organize this surprise? Because I love it."

Nero chuckled, and Bee darted to his side, stealing Autumn into her arms before breaking into baby talk.

Movement drew my attention to my side, and I turned as Santos emerged from the room, too.

"Boo!" he said and laughed.

I dragged him into my arms, my throat tightening. "You were part of this, weren't you? Plus, what's Bee been feeding you, you're taller than me."

He grinned. "Bee's barely home. But her dad is a mean cook and has taken me on as an apprentice for his inventions."

"Does that mean you won't be working with me anymore?" I frowned.

He stared at the room, then back at me. "You couldn't get

rid of me. Especially with all the new fixtures. You need someone to run this place."

My heart soared at having everyone close to me together.

"Okay, who wants some wicked tea?" Bee called out from across the shop, and Santos darted into the storage room and came back out with two platters of cakes.

"Whoa, who's been baking?" I asked and stared straight at Nero, who winked back at me.

With Dagen making his way to the food, I took Jay into my arms and joined the merriment. Because this was what life was about. Spending time with loved ones, laughing, and kissing my little babies. I looked down at Jay, his eyes the color of the greenest fields, and I ran a finger down his nose.

Nero dashed into the storeroom and returned with a carriage wide enough for all three babies in his arms. Blankets layered the inside.

"See, I made something, too. It means if we're at the store or at your grandma's place in the woods, the triplets have somewhere to sleep." He smirked, and I placed Jay inside. Bee and Oryn did the same, and my three babies lay there, Jay still snoozing, Autumn kicking her arms and legs, and Alexy sucking her thumb.

Each already had their own personality and had captured my heart. Just as my three shifters had. They hugged me as we all stood around staring down at our family. Yep, this might not have been the future I'd planned, with three men and being a wolf, but it was better than I could have ever imagined.

And with a glance at my painting, I could have sworn it felt as if Grandma was with us, too.

ABOUT MILA YOUNG

Bestselling author, Mila Young tackles everything with the zeal and bravado of the fairytale heroes she grew up reading about. She slays monsters, real and imaginary, like there's no tomorrow. By day she rocks a keyboard as a marketing extraordinaire. At night she battles with her might pen-sword, creating fairytale retellings, and sexy ever after tales. In her spare time, she loves pretending she's a mighty warrior, walks on the beach with her dogs, cuddling up with her cats, and devouring every fantasy tale she can get her pinkies on.

Ready for the next story from Mila Young? Subscribe today: www.subscribepage.com/milayoung

Mila Young loves to connect with readers.

For more information...
milayoungauthor@gmail.com
www.facebook.com/milayoungauthor
twitter.com/MilaYoungAuthor